With Love & be
[handwritten signature]

WATCHWORDS

SIXTEEN SHORT STORIES

PHILIP NEAL

July 2018

*For Jonathan Jnr, Victoria, Justine, Jonathan Snr,
Isobel, and Martin, of Antique Watch Company,
Clerkenwell, London.*

Contents

Zenith Nadir

Cyclops

Paint Job

Gunner Saddler Yates

The Tranquillity of Copernicus

Death to Spies

Flight

Our Song is Love Unknown

Strange Odyssey

Homeland

Palm Sunday

To Bernard from Mary, 1939

A Fine Timepiece

Nineteen seventy-nine

The Smoke That Thunders

Dedication

Prologue

In 2009 I lost a watch through a hole in a pocket lining. It was perhaps like the hole Alice fell into, as it led me to a wonderland. I owned two watches, but the lost one was special. A friend had admired it and said it looked like a Cartier from the 1930s. As a counsellor, I would say what I did next was dysfunctional. I didn't grieve and accept my loss. Instead I set out with determination to replace what had gone. I bought several watches which resembled the Festina in one way or another. That led to me noticing others I liked. I think I had amassed about thirty when, one day, I was on eBay and there was the exact match of the lost watch. The quest over, I lost interest in watches.

All the watches I had were new, battery powered, quartz movement timepieces. Retro, but not vintage. In 2015 I decided I wanted a 1939 vintage watch as a birthday present. No special reason, except I had been fascinated by the year all my adult life: the onset of dystopia, and the high water mark in several areas of human endeavour before the post-war period.

I managed to buy a piece of junk on eBay. It came from the home country of Paddington Bear. What to do? I Googled vintage watch repairers, and went for the most convenient, close to where I was working. Antique Watch Company is in Clerkenwell, which I now know was the throbbing heart of Britain's vanished watch making industry. The shop is an old curiosity, but the staff certainly aren't. Jon, the manager, listed all the things wrong with my trophy. This meant I could return it for refund with professional evidence.

I soon became friends with AWC, which had unfortunate effects on my bank balance, but brought me a new passion in the form of collecting vintage watches; the only collecting I've done since postage stamps as a boy (on the whole watches cost more). Jon asked me if I'd write a review of AWC on Google. I was very happy to do this. When he saw it, he came up with the suggestion we might write something together.

A few months later I had a dream in which one of my watches was involved in the narrative of a murder. One of two streams which led to this book had begun flowing.

The second was that I had wanted for several years to try writing fiction. I had been an academic anthropologist, and had published, but I wanted to get away from the strictures of academic writing. I had no idea if I was capable, so I chose to do a beginners' fiction course. Fortunately I felt encouraged by the feedback from others and so I waited for inspiration. It came from the dream. All my watches were without context. Who had owned them, where had they been, what had they seen? The first I bought from Jon was a 1916 officer's trench watch. It was 2016 and the Somme was very much in people's minds. My grandfather had fought in World War, but he died four years before I was born, and I knew little about him. Like many other serving men, he didn't talk to his family about his war experiences. An imaginative recreation could bring my grandfather alive for me, with research at the National Archives in Kew to fill in details from his service record and the unit diaries of his brigade. The watch could be a device to mark an emotionally significant event on the battlefield.

I soon realized that a set of stories in each of which a watch played an integral role would be difficult to write, liable to repetition, and

Prologue   3

potentially tedious to read. Instead I looked at and thought about the watches, and the first idea that came I used as the touch paper for a story. It could be as little as the make of watch. Thus Zenith Nadir, the first story I wrote, and the first in this collection.

I hope you will enjoy these stories, though some are in a dark emotional register. I realized in the middle of writing that the stories were distinct, but there was an autobiographical thread which linked a number of them. I was a man in his fifties reflecting on significant events in his life.

I hope some of you may gain an interest in vintage watches. They are endlessly varied, aesthetic objects which also do something useful. Each story is preceded by a photograph of the watch which inspired it, with a brief description which points to its link with the story.

Zenith Pilot, 1960s, stainless steel, Switzerland, mechanical movement. This watch has a California dial, distinguished by Roman numerals above the 3-9 axis, Arabic numerals below, and an inverted triangle at 12. These dials were invented by Rolex in the 1930s. After the end of the war a large number had their dials restored in California, hence the name. There's a caveat – the dial on this watch has been restored and its style may not be like the original.

Zenith Nadir

My ears sing in the gentle buffet of sea breeze. I contemplate my tea, my mother. Is this harmony, her and I, and where we are?

Above the reed beds a single marsh harrier perches in the air, talons ready to shred the oblivious vole below. The rare raptor seems to shimmer to those with their binoculars hidden in the hide. The wide expanse of marsh, heath, wood and shingle bank are what the twins have so longed to see. Once before, their care home brought them here for a day. Most of the children didn't seem to know what to do. Streetwise, with the Fagin-taught skills of acquisition, a cow was still a large and worrisome creature for them, looking you in the eye as if plotting an attack. They didn't trust the people either, with their binoculars for spying, huge cameras to sneak photos, and a strange uniform of dark green waxed coats.

Growing up with the other, older children had been difficult for Dan and Tracy, older brother and younger sister. They'd been told that Tracy had something called autism, and she felt different and differently treated. They didn't know what autism meant. Or retard. Some of the other children were cruel to Tracy, so having Dan meant survival for both.

That earlier day trip brought something to life in Tracy, which gave her an eagerness for today. Dan heard the birds that time, sea gulls cay caying, the hoot of an insomniac owl, the twitters among the reeds. For Tracy it was what she saw that had been so special. The little birds were not all the same. Some brown, some blue and yellow, and a flash of steely blue diving into the water.

"It's a kingfisher," her brother said.

He knew what to give her for her birthday. While she was not looking he sneaked into the shop and bought her a book on British birds. She read this from cover to cover several times, and the nicely battered book she felt tenderly in her pocket on this second trip. Bullfinch, blue tit, reed warbler, pied flycatcher. She could name them all, as she made a tick on the right page in the book. These birds were utter enchantment to her. Not like the greedy grey pigeons in the city which looked stupid even if the man on TV said they weren't. Dan asked her if she wished she could fly?

"Don't be stupid, Dan, I don't have any wings."

This day Tracy wanted to walk up the shingle bank to see the sea and the bird reserve at the same time. One of the carers said yes and they trudged up the shingle bank, one foot slowly after another, rolling back a bit in between. This only made Tracy more determined to get to the top. The wind now whipped faster round her face, bringing a tingle of salt spray. The sea was brown, like some of the birds. She would have preferred blue, but life couldn't be perfect. In the distance was a very odd sight. There was something that looked like a factory, but parked on the beach. Behind it was an enormous white golf ball. Is there a giants' golf course, she wondered. Dan caught her eye and said "It's a nuclear power station."

Zenith Nadir   7

"Oh." Tracy wasn't enlightened. But it wasn't what interested her. She turned again inland. A huge and majestic heron flew over like a feathered pterodactyl. And Dan heard the booming of a bittern in the reeds, something he'd read about in Tracy's book.

"I want to go down to the scrape, Dan". Tracy knew this was where she would find her treasure. Here nested the avocet, the symbol of the RSPB ("Royal Society for the Protection of Birds", she said out loud). The group moved on together once some of the teenagers had stopped stoning each other with pebbles. Martha was told to run after her Haribo packet and Diet Coke can, even though they were blowing away fast. She complied after her tiny performance of feeling oppressed failed to gain further attention.

There they were, smart black and white and elegant, with thin cornflower-blue legs and beautiful black upcurving bills. The man on TV called them the Audrey Hepburn of the bird world. This didn't mean anything to Tracy but Joe, their oldest carer, said he'd meant Audrey Hepburn in *My Fair Lady*. Joe often said very strange things, and Tracy put this down to his being over forty and about to die, his brain first.

Tracy was enthralled as she watched the birds strutting like ballerinas on their toes, and was so excited when she managed to spot some eggs, so hard to see among the stones. She smiled and gesticulated, and Dan knew she was truly happy on this day, as he had so wanted her to be. And then a moment of perfection for him too. A very small, undistinguished bird rose into the air and continued rising vertically, as if pulled up by the beam of an alien spacecraft. Then the melody began, a heavenward, joyful twittering, as if for the sheer joy of being alive. Dan drew in and held a long breath. For a moment the world was a perfect place to be. Sea, sun, birdsong, zephyr. The skylark had attained its zenith. "Ah, Vaughan Williams," said Joe.

My tea's cold. I wasn't enjoying it anyway. Or anything else. Mum is pretending we're having a nice day out, but her distracted look betrays she isn't feeling it. I cannot experience any pleasure. Not being with Mum, not being in this place on such a day, though I know I otherwise love coming here.

My depressions are a trial for us both. First I have to stop work, then I descend into an abyss where all I want is oblivion, and this often comes in a bottle. I lose motivation even to shave and shower, and feeding myself is a struggle. If someone asks me what it feels like to be depressed, I say that it isn't so much a feeling as a total inability to feel anything. Like being dead. You can wander the world wraith-like looking at everyone else getting on with life, but you are in exile. There is a painting by Munch (no surprise), which connects with depression for me better than any attempt to harness it with words. It's not "The Scream". It's "The Dance of Life". A woman looks on as a group of people dance happily. She is distraught, excluded, unremarked on. It's in the National Gallery in Oslo if you are ever there.

One day follows another in rigid monotony. There's the anxiety too, like a dripping tap of adrenaline, dripping to eternity. This is why people kill themselves; I know this now.

My mother feeds me and I feel guilty for feeling I am infantilised by this. I also feel guilty for being dependent like a child again, when I am forty and she is seventy.

Zenith Nadir   9

We sit in the sun and look at each other. I attempt conversation but the effort is too much. This is a magical place. I know this but can't feel it. It's as if someone has taken a black and white print and reversed it into a ghostly negative image. This can't be worse than sitting in the house, but the setting means the contrast between a "normal" day here and a "depressed" day is almost too hard to bear.

We amble through the woods and cross the marshes. This is dejection, a state where everything is the same. Some elderly people pass and greet us in the friendly country manner. One of them makes a mistake which neither of us can bear to contradict. She thought we were husband and wife. I'm not sure why this is so disturbing.

I help Mum up the shingle bank. We turn our backs to the wind. Down by the scrape a girl is pointing and everyone looks up. A speck, almost invisible until it is against the blue, rising, rising, trilling. A skylark. This is my worst moment. It may as well have been a crow.

Longines mystery watch, 10 Carat white gold filled, 1960s, Switzerland, mechanical movement.
The watch has only one hand. Mystery watches are a diversion first patented by Hugues Rime in 1889. They vary as to how cryptically they display the time.

Cyclops

I'm slightly out of breath. Rudely awakened at nine to get here for eleven. I go into the office. Marcus is already here, pretending to be preoccupied with business.

"Your 11 a.m. client Bella phoned in to cancel. She's had to go away at short notice. I've written the details on a Post-it over there."

I look at the note.

"Oh no."

I had anticipated the moment. Bella is seventy, so her mother is ancient, though youthfully cantankerous. She only gave up driving after hitting the village pillar box and giving the finger to the postie she'd almost killed.

"Thank you, Marcus, I'll be prepared for what to say when she comes next week."

The time arrives. It's an anniversary of my fiftieth birthday, so I put on the watch my partner chose for me then. It is lovely. It was made the same year as me. It's a Longines. It draws out my occasional paranoia.

It's a mystery dial watch, and it was endless fun for my partner that it took me a week to learn how to tell the time with it. It only has one hand and I thought the others had fallen off.

I arrive at work solemn but not too funereal.

I distract myself in the counselling room online, then slam my Chromebook shut on Facebook as a firm rapping comes at the door. She's always on time. I have my own theory that analysing the quality and volume of door knock, scratch, whack or kick could make therapy a lot quicker and cheaper. And safer, were there a key. Of course I make allowances, for the hearing impaired, and those who turn up on the wrong day or week. I'm sure Bella was a PE teacher in a previous life, though she's never raised the subject.

She strides in.

"Come in, Bella, I'm pleased to see you."

"Well, it's been quite a week."

"Yes, Marcus gave me your message. I'm really sorry about your loss."

"I'm feeling distraught now. She was so important to me, the only thing which had really been a constant in my life. I'd had her for nearly twelve years."

Cyclops

"I thought you said she was ninety-two?"

Bella knits her brows with an "are you mad?" expression in her eyes.

"No, no, no, my labradoodle Pixie has died."

I brush off the mental image of a sketch of a fairy's labia. I don't know much about dogs.

"Bella, I'm sorry, I have to ask, what's a labradoodle?"

"It's a cross betw… My dog died. My mother's in hospital, I went to visit her."

I briefly entertain fantasies of decapitating Marcus.

"I'm so sorry I got that wrong, Bella. Looks like the message I received wasn't the one you left."

"It certainly was not."

I notice the embryo of a smile on Bella's lips, much to my relief. I thought she was going to eat me.

Bella and I then explore whether she would rather it were her mother or her dog who had died.

At the end of the day Marcus is alone in the office.

"I could gladly kill you."

"Why?" One eyebrow raised, his sarcastic Vivien Leigh, as I call it.

"That message you gave me last week about Bella."

"Yes?"

"It was her dog that had died, not her mother."

Marcus begins to shake before I grant him permission.

"Don't you fucking laugh. That was the most embarrassing moment I've ever had with a client."

Cyclops

(That's not quite true. That was when a psychosexual patient showed me his green painted penis, unsolicited. As a green therapist myself I was lucky this man's reputation went before him and I wasn't suspended.)

"Hold on, hold on, bunny boiler, here's the message."

He hands me a Post-it: "Bella won't be able to come to her appointment today. She's very upset about her dog dying, and her mother is going to hospital for some tests so she needs to travel there today."

Marcus adds: "You must have taken the wrong Post-it. I pointed out the correct one. It was in your favourite royal purple."

"You bolloxing uphill-gardening lying bastard, that is *not* what happened. You must have swapped the messages. You know what she's like. I was expecting to be crucified, then hidden under the floorboards and forgotten about. Remember. I'm updating that list of your psychopathic traits."

"As a Transactionalist I hardly need indicate you're in child ego state now."

"Oh piss off and die, Marcus."

"Rude."

"Please piss off, then." I'm on a roll but Marcus hasn't returned me the ball and serves me an awkward bounce.

"I've got a good idea. In two weeks they are starting a paranoia group here. I think you might find it helpful. Your outbursts are getting worse, so you'll be sleeping in the spare room tonight. I've even washed the bedclothes since your last self-exile."

I'd rather eat my own head than let Marcus get the last word. I always end up feeling like a cockroach under his heel.

A great put-down comes to me.

"When I get home I'm going to edit your CV. I'm going to put 'Exalted Cyclops, KKK' under Positions of Responsibility. That's a promotion since Grand Dragon. And if you ever get that FRSA you so much want, you'll get MRSA instead. Oh, and your favourite novel is *The Piddle of the Sands* by Foreskin Childers."

"Finished?"

I jump through the door, with the gleeful thrill of anticipated evil doings. So much of my life is devoted to being good I just need a naughty moment every now and then.

Cyclops

I'll go back to my watch shop, Chronology, and see how much they think I can get for the Longines. Then I can have a watch with three hands which I will understand and Marcus will be forced to see.

Bugger, bugger, buggery. He got the last word. Again.

Sturmanskie (Navigator) commemorating Yuri Gagarin as the first man in space on 12 April 1961, circa 1980s-1990s, stainless steel, USSR, mechanical movement. Gagarin wore a Sturmanskie in space, alas not this one.

Paint Job

I remembered Dad's watchmaker being somewhere near Saffron Hill. It was a still, warm day, so I was happy to wander. About twenty minutes later, there it was, on a corner. Chronology. I walked into the door then saw the buzzer. Inside there was already a customer at the counter. A man wearing Bermuda shorts, silk shirt and deck shoes. A bit optimistic for April.

"I've forgotten to bring it, but it's that Glashutte you sold me about two years ago. It isn't working," the man says.

"Any ideas why not?" asks the watchmaker.

"The hands aren't moving and there's water inside, which shouldn't be there. I was testing it for German efficiency of manufacture."

"And how did you do that?"

"I took it for a swim. It says stossgesichert on the back, which is German for waterproof."

"Does it also say Wasserdicht?"

20   Watchwords

"Not sure. The point is I knew the chlorine could be toxic so I thought fast and put it in the microwave when I got home. Just for a minute, on defrost."

"What do you do for a living?"

"I own twenty-four boats ... What can you do about my watch?"

"Very little. It's unlikely ever to work again. And it's out of warranty."

"That's ridiculous."

"Yes, it is. I can't do anything for you. Would you take your iPhone for a swim?"

"Of course not. Don't be ridiculous."

"Goodbye, sir."

"I was going to say that first. You won't be seeing me again."

"Likewise."

Paint Job

After witnessing this exchange I'm feeling a bit nervous. Fortunately things brighten up when the watchmaker turns to his assistant to say, "You can take Mr Grumpy off our death row customer list, Cat."

"Good, Joel, that only leaves twelve."

"How can I help?" To my relief it's Cat who says this.

"I have this watch I've just inherited from my dad. I think it may be very rare; at least that's what it said when he bought it on eBay."

"What make is it?" This time it's Joel.

"Sturmanskie."

"Can you read that sign?"

"Yes. Are you an optician too?"

"No. What does it say?"

"We don't repair Russian watches."

"Why is that?"

"Like their politics, the Soviet watch movements were crude. Or crap, to use the technical term."

Even I could tell the conversation wasn't going well, until I remembered.

"Silly me, it's working perfectly well. I just wondered how much it might be worth. I've got someone to translate what's on the dial for me. Down here it says '12 April 1961, Yuri Gagarin.'"

"Does it also say 'Wore me in space'?"

"No."

"It's a commemorative watch, it could have been made any time between 1961 and now. Value – maybe twenty quid on a good day."

Oh dear, not what I thought I would hear.

"I've noticed it glows in the dark."

"Yes, they often used luminous paint on the hands and numerals so

Paint Job 23

you could tell the time in the dark."

"What made it luminous?"

"The radioactivity."

"The what?"

"The paint glowed because of the radium in it. You know, the stuff that killed Marie Curie."

"I know you can't repair it, but could you put a longer strap on it for me?"

"Yes, that's no problem, it's only the intestines we won't deal with, Mr ...?

"Carfax."

I chose a nice lizard skin strap, and a canvas military one. I hoped I wouldn't one day become a pacifist vegetarian. I left the shop, and made my way straight home, knowing now what my tragic life needed next.

I went straight on Google and typed in "Luminous Watch Paint." Not many people were selling it, but I bought the largest container I could find.

The sex clinic

It's the Wednesday lunchtime team meeting. I will be finishing my placement in the psychosexual clinic soon, but I can take on one more patient. The discussion has come round to the last patient to be allocated.

My supervisor, Dr Eden, is holding the new patient folders.

"This gentleman, Walter Carfax, is thirty-four and has been referred by his Community Mental Health Team. He started using mental health services following panic attacks after an incident of self-harm ten years ago, described as having a sexual basis. I'm afraid it doesn't say more on this. They are referring him now for suicidal thoughts resulting from his sex drive. He has told them that he has performed an act of sexual self-mutilation which fell short of an actual attempt to take his own life, but which he had worked out in considerable detail. He's done something to his penis. They are referring him to us as they find the sexual aspects of his behaviour difficult to understand and alarming. All his attempts at self-harm have a sexual aspect, but he refuses to discuss this with them. He sounds interesting. Who has space to see him?"

I seize the opportunity.

Paint Job 25

"If no one else minds, I would like to see him, as I won't be able to take on any new clients after today."

Everyone assents to this.

"Don't forget," adds Dr Eden, "we're having a rare visit from Professor Greatorex then, and I'm sure his input will be useful."

There are some raised eyebrows. I haven't met the Professor before, the man who set up the clinic, but I've heard plenty. He's described as "brisk", "striking", and "direct". Not euphemisms. Our soon-to-retire senior doctor Manic Max had never hit it off with him and referred to him as General Fieldmouse-Gurring. We knew about the discreet spelling because he always attached a tag to his Secret Santa contribution. So far the Prof had managed not to draw it. Manic Max's hobby was an interest in probability.

"All right, let's go and do some work."

I believe in being on time so I don't hang around with the consultants finding ways to waste theirs in the admin office. Usually the conversation is about who's going to Dubai, the Algarve, or about to risk death through dangerous sports, including golf.

I put my head round the door of the waiting room. Several patients are sitting at the other end of the room, looking a little nervous. "Mr

Carfax?"

Someone I hadn't noticed, because he's on his own and next to me, stands up, and I take him through to the consulting room.

"Mr Carfax, I'm Philip Neal, and I'm a trainee psychotherapist."

"Couldn't they find someone more senior for me?"

"This is an initial assessment. If you have complex needs you might see a consultant psychiatrist in future."

Walter seemed pleased with this.

"First, Mr Carfax, I need to ask you to take the balaclava off."

"Why? I was really nervous about people seeing me coming to a sex problems clinic so I wanted to be as inconspicuous as possible."

"I don't think the balaclava is helping. The point is it's illegal to wear one in public. With all those people killed by the bombs on the tube last week, don't you think you might frighten people too?"

"Oh, that's why they looked nervous in the waiting room. All right, I'll take it off."

Paint Job   27

"Thank you. I understand that you've done something harmful to yourself, to your penis, because of your sex drive."

"That's right."

"Do you mean because your sex drive is so high you feel tormented and in danger of offending?"

"No, the opposite. I have no sex drive at all. My penis has given me no pleasure whatsoever, so I decided to kill it."

"I need to ask you, are you still having thoughts about harming yourself or anyone else, or taking your own life?"

"No, I'm not."

"So how did this all start, Mr Carfax?"

"I was becoming very depressed with my penis. Most men seem to have a good relationship with theirs, almost like with an old friend. Called Percy. And they get a lot of excitement too. I never have. Mine has been a terrible disappointment to me. So I decided to liquidate it. Well, not just it, all of me, but starting with my penis, my greatest source of distress. I wasn't going to cut it off or anything like that as that would have been too quick and merciful."

"Painful too."

"I wouldn't mind the pain, but I'd have bled to death and that would have been too quick, and I didn't want to leave Mrs Stafford will a large cleaning bill."

At this point I felt I'd walked as far as that point in a swimming pool where I either had to swim or drown, and I'd forgotten my water wings.

"I got my idea from visiting the watch repairers. They were telling me about how the paint on watches which glows in the dark contains radium. It's radioactive. It killed Marie Curie. I thought, what if I get some paint and paint my penis with it? It will probably die a slow and horrible death. It would be like a mini Nagasaki. Would you like to see? I haven't washed it for three weeks so you can still see the paint."

"NO, Mr Carfax, only a doctor or …"

Too late. He had stood, dropped his trousers, no underwear, and I could see his pale green ring. A ring. Only his foreskin appeared to have been painted.

"Please pull your trousers back up now, Mr Carfax."

Paint Job   29

To my great relief he did so.

"It was a failure. After a few days nothing had happened. I felt too depressed to kill myself."

Wednesday comes round again, with the promised presence of Professor Greatorex.

I've just repeated what Mr Carfax told me. Professor Greatorex has been silent so far, but is turning purple.

"Cunting hell."

This isn't quite what I was expecting.

"That's enough arseholing. This is the third time Mr Carfax has succeeded in getting referred to us. By some miracle he hasn't discovered he can self-refer. If any of you ever tells him he can refer himself I will personally flay you.

"I think he's got hold of a copy of DSM IV and either swallowed it or is choosing a disorder from each chapter. The first time he came he'd developed a phobia of *vagina dentata*."

"What's that?" I ask.

"Cunted tooth … toothed cunt! Doesn't exist. A man's fear of having his cock bitten off by a toothed vagina. Cultural mythology. A leader's way of controlling sexual behaviour in his underlings. Mind you, in this case, if Mr Carfax had lost it to the Streatham Snapper or whoever he wouldn't be troubling us now."

"I think my wife's got one," chips in Max.

"Then it's a pity she hasn't used it," replies Greatorex.

"Second referral of Mr Carfax. He had developed an obsession with women's breasts. Not one where he would be guilty of sexual assault, as he assured me. No, he wanted the convenience of growing a pair of female breasts of his own. He'd begun to inject cow's milk behind his nipples. Self-harm.

"The CMHT cack themselves every time they hear cock or vag, hence the referrals. This man is self-harming, bizarrely I admit, but self-harming. Third referral, he says he's tried unsuccessfully to murder his penis. He doesn't have a psychosexual problem."

I venture that he's in distress and has complex problems. This seems to stop the Prof in his tracks, to my amazement.

"'Complex.' Now that's useful. One thought first. Did it strike you as odd, Philip, that he'd only painted his foreskin?"

Paint Job 31

"Yes, though he had said he wanted it to be a very slow suicide."

"Here's what I think. By only painting his prepuce he thought that if it really did begin to wither he could have been saved by a circumcision, rather than complete gender reassignment surgery. Suicide with an-opt out.

"Complex, that's the word, Philip. Let's find a complex needs group to refer him to. He will be flattered by the title, and not know that it's psychiatric short-hand for 'pains in the arse'. If he's lucky there'll be a couple of psychopaths in the group, and that might direct his fantasy life away from mental health services."

"Are you sure there's no psychiatric or psychological problem?" says Deirdre, a secret fan of Melanie Klein.

"He's a time-wasting fantasist. Will that do?"

Later in the afternoon I see Dr Eden in the corridor.

"I'm sorry we didn't get to speak before that. Would you like a 'debrief' now?"

"Yes, I think I need it."

32   Watchwords

"You mustn't take the Prof's language too seriously. His bearing comes from a military background. His father had a very distinguished career in the army, and was decorated for his services on D-Day. Unfortunately his decorations later extended to Waterloo, Agincourt and the Battle of Hastings. I think the later victories may have compensated for his general dislike of the French, whom he blamed for later problems with the Germans. When the Alzheimer's worsened, Juno, his son, whom you've just met, had to cope with that, as well as a brother who was bipolar.

"He went on to become an army psychiatrist. Before his first posting overseas things were rather quiet. It was before the legalisation allowing LGBT people to serve in the armed forces, so following some rumours, they asked him to uncover homosexuals. He asked what he was supposed to do and they just said 'You're the psychiatrist.' Apparently he added, 'Shall I hide under their fucking beds?'

"He was posted to Afghanistan, to Helmand. Things went well for a while, but then he started behaving strangely, and feared that the family misfortune had arrived to take him too. He was inundated with PTSD cases and the strain and dissociation transferred onto him.

"One day, someone heard him talking outside. He was saying something like, 'What do you prefer, Hastings, cock or cunt?'"

"Is that how he usually addressed his men?"

Paint Job

"Oh, ha. No, Hastings was a dog. The regimental mascot. It was a stray which had adopted them. Harold named him in honour of his father."

"It was time for him to come home, and Hastings came with him. It took a while for him to recover, but he went on to set up the clinic. Now there are occasional complaints when he says cunt, but the paperwork always mysteriously disappears. They say that Max hates only one person in the clinic more than Prof Greatorex, and that's Deirdre, whom he suspects of the complaints."

The next week

I must go and collect my watch. I'd rushed out of the shop to go on eBay so hadn't waited for them to fit a strap. Mr Neal has told me that the Professor is referring me to a Complex Needs Group. At last they seem to be taking me seriously. The CMHT only ask if I'd harmed myself again.

I press the buzzer and Cat lets me in.

"I'll just get Joel for you. He said he'd like to see you when you come in."

"I've just come to collect my watch and the two straps."

Joel comes down from the workshop.

"Ah, Mr Carfax, you've come to collect Yuri Gagarin's watch?"

"That's right."

"Here you are. It looks good on the lizard. And here's the canvas NATO strap. A Soviet watch will go really well with that."

"I'm glad you think so. There's something else I wanted to ask. You know you were telling me about radium paint on old watches. Is it really dangerous?"

"No, you'd probably need to sleep with the watch in your ear for a thousand years. The amount of radium is minute. The people who would have suffered were the people who painted the dials. They probably licked the brush in between each stroke. Some of them were known to die from it.

"The other thing is that radium paint isn't used any more. If you buy luminous watch paint now, the glowing comes from tritium. It's totally harmless."

"Oh, so watches are all harmless now?"

"Yes, but there's one exception. Many watches used to be chrome

Paint Job　　　　35

plated, like old car bumpers. Every now and then Toxic Tim comes round for rechroming jobs and we all have to hide."

"Why?"

"The material used in chrome respraying is highly toxic, and the person doing it has to take lots of precautions. The spray contains cyanide."

I paid and left the shop swiftly. My next grand project lay ahead of me.

Silver half-hunter officer's trench watch, 1916, Wilson and Gill, 139-141 Regents Street, London, mechanical movement. Wrist watches like these, as opposed to pocket watches, were introduced for French troops in 1915 to make it easier to tell the time while carrying weapons and equipment in both hands.

Gunner Saddler Yates

Italicised text is taken verbatim from the unit diaries of the 34th reserve battery, 277 Brigade, Royal Field Artillery. I also consulted my grandfather's service record, partly destroyed by fire during Luftwaffe bombing in the Blitz. With thanks to the National Archives, Kew.

Shoreditch 1900

The stench the shouting the punching down Shoreditch High Street. Even this isn't so bad on a sunny day. Today's grey. Houndsditch is where they threw dead dogs. Mad Harry the philosopher who sits by the statue says Shoreditch meant Sewer Ditch to the Anglo Saxons. No kidding. And that was fucking hundreds of years ago. Not much change.

Queen Vic's got to kick the bucket soon. Something must change or we'll be rioting. News from South Africa, we're being knocked out by the Boers. That's what they say. Bits of newspaper that get to us say it's all heroism for the British Empire. Is Shoreditch in the British Empire?

I get back to our two up two down and Mum shoves my head in a bucket of water.

"You stink."

"What doesn't round here?"

She's always reminding me how lucky I am with an apprenticeship and a trade to follow. Dad drank himself to death. At least I can't be down the pub. Course the pubs was still full of children drinking then.

Have you been to a tannery? Once it was harder work, but they used what nature provided. Now it's chromium salts. It's killing us. Factory owners won't admit it. We're dying so fine ladies and gentlemen can buy their shoes up West. Poor women sell us dog turds for the recipe.

Shoreditch 1902

I'm at the end of my apprenticeship at last. Working the leather, cutting, stitching, finishing, admiring. I can look at something and say Fred made that, and it's good. Them up West can go fuck themselves. What I really want is to do something for the people, people like me in the East End, who can't fight their corner. I've always loved horses, and they like me in return. I'm going to be a saddler.

Woolwich Barracks 1916

King and Country. I've done my best to give them the V sign. Some things have changed around home mind. We've been cut off in the East End. Literally. Transport was unreliable and we didn't have good connections to other bits of London. A trip up West was get there, turn

Gunner Saddler Yates 39

round and come back again. The working classes weren't getting much representation – the Liberals and Tories were in charge of everything. We knew of some things which happened, like Annie Besant and the Match Girls' strike back when I was born, but she wasn't a working-class girl. The trades unions began, something to protect working men and women at last, though it didn't expand to my trade. We began to feel we had some muscle, and before the war I joined the British Socialist Party.

At first I felt nothing. Let three imperial cousins butcher each other. Of course, I soon realised they were using their ordinary men like me to slay each other. I wasn't following that moustached prick Kitchener. The law was likely to change soon so I knew by spring 1916 I would have to join up, go into hiding, or be a conchie. I couldn't decide which.

I took Mum and my sisters Nancy and Edie up West for a day out before I chose my fate. We walked in Hyde Park, up Piccadilly and into Regent Street. It could have been a different planet from the East End. Something caught my eye in the window of a gold and silversmith's shop. A beautiful silver watch. You could see the hands with the lid shut, or open it to see the full dial. The French troops had demanded a replacement for cumbersome pocket watches. The new kind, like the one in the window, was called a wristwatch. How I'd love something such as this, but I might as well wish for the king's crown. Still I looked up quickly for the shop name and address –

Wilson and Gill, 139–141 Regent Street.

I made the easiest decision; to become one of the herd. I couldn't stand prison, being white feathered, or spat on as a conchie. My special skill,

I knew, would keep me out of the trenches. I decided to join up, and came forward on 9 July 1916. We'd moved up a bit in the world, to Dalston, up the Kingsland Road. I was earning a bit by then, and if I'd absconded the family would have been destitute.

I got taken on at Woolwich Barracks. For the duration, as far as I know, I'm in 34th reserve battery, 277 Brigade, Royal Field Artillery. I get my certificate of trade proficiency as a skilled saddler. I will make boots for the men as well as tack for the horses.

Looking back at my service record now, I think I'll keep quiet about my field hospital admissions. Once for toothache and once for haemorrhoids. Not heroism, but most heroes didn't make it to hospital.

France 1917

It's almost Christmas by the time we leave for France. Can't tell as we file on board if there's more excitement or fear. Fear. The Somme has just finished. Mum and Edie and Nancy are on the dockside waving. The tears behind the masks. Mine are stifled, by fear, sadness, anger.

We arrive in Boulogne after a smooth crossing. The quiet makes it worse. I arrive on 21 December 1916. It will be exactly two years and two months before my return. I'm to face the worst winter of my life, for the men and horses.

Gunner Saddler Yates

Our locations have to remain secret. Each day the officer in command makes a diary entry. We could not see these. You can now.

21 January General Fanshawe and Brigadier Ward attended Church Parade and thanked men for prior service.

Pair of patronising cunts. We've done what God wants, and if the next battle is carnage it'll be the same, only a bit more solemn. Pack up your troubles they used to sing. No fucking paper or string now.

26 January, frost, men and officers in billets, horses in open. Very cold. March on Fouilloy. No fuel of any kind available.

At least they get us indoors as well as the officers. I can't bear what it's like for the horses. I go out and give them a brushing, coaxing, soothing, as they stand there shivering, terrified. Startled eyes. In the mist there's another figure.

"Who's there?" he cries.

"Gunner Yates."

"Ah, our saddler."

"Yes, sir."

42   Watchwords

"What do you think of all this, Yates?" I wonder if there's a trap, so I say, "It's miserable for us. Worse for the horses. Look in their eyes, sir. Poor beasts can't possibly know why they are here."

Captain Hoath then made an extraordinary gesture. He put his arms around his stallion's neck and rested his head against it. A gear in my head shifted and would never reverse. This was the first gesture of true kindness I had seen from an officer. I didn't mind it was to a horse. I love them too.

"Oslo, you must survive this winter, boy."

Oslo was the horse's name, because of Copenhagen, the Duke of Wellington's steed at Waterloo.

"I can understand why most of you men hate us, Yates. We command, you follow. One officer down, then dominoes of men. The British Empire. I'm a little Englander. I want no empire, I want humanity."

I am so astonished by this I find nothing to say. He must be taking the piss, or risking ridicule when I tell the others.

"Yes, I went to public school like the other officers, but mine was Leighton Park, founded by the Quakers. We believe in equality and being responsible for our own ideas about the world. What's your name, Gunner?"

Gunner Saddler Yates   43

"Yates."

"No, I meant your first name."

"Fred."

"May I call you that?"

"Yes, sir."

"And I'm Horace. We can address each other thus out of earshot. What is it you want for the future, Fred?"

"First, this war must stop. I'm sick of being pig swill for the Empire. I became a socialist before the war. Some of what I want is the same as the Quakers, only without God."

"I've heard about socialism, Fred. I even agree with some of it. I bet that surprises you? I'm not sure what God is, Fred. Not here on this frozen sod in France. I listen to the Padre's homilies but it all seems like a pantomime. If you're a socialist, Fred, how can you stand being here in the service of a king?"

"No choice. My family would be left destitute, my father's long dead. I'm twenty-eight, not married, God knows if I will ever have my own family. What about you?"

"Same. No wife, no children. It spooks me sometimes. I'm an only child. If I don't make it back from here and marry my line dies out."

"There might be a point to the fighting, sir. Horace. These monarchs might prove to be their own downfall. I hear there is a movement in Russia to overthrow the Tsar and replace him with a proletariat."

"What's that?"

"A government of the people by the people."

20 March 1917. Officers and men at wagon lines out every night – work so very trying and exacting. Teams taking up ammunition shelled and several casualties.

This is Fred Yates's birthday.

"Dear Mum,

I'm twenty-nine today. I can't say how it is here, because of the censor. I can say that my pride in my work remains. Many of the men have

Gunner Saddler Yates 45

new boots I've made. Their sores and blisters are healing. At last some dubbin came through with the supplies so their feet aren't soaking wet. Right now the ground is still frozen, so at least the mud's reduced.

It's the poor horses I feel worst for. Outside all the time. Starving, freezing, dying. I'm keeping their tack repaired so we can keep riding and the teams can pull the heavy guns. They say something big is coming.

Love to you, Nancy and Edie,

Your son,

Fred

Vimy Ridge, April 2017

2 April 1917. North of the Vimy Ridge. Weather very bad. Trying for horses and men. Enemy opened heavy artillery fire on trenches of the 4th Canadian division.

9 April 1917. Attack by Canadians on Vimy Ridge. All objectives gained.

The Canadian Fourth Division have joined us and we all feel cheered. We hope at last to take Vimy Ridge, and something called the Pimple, because of its shape. It's still winter and the conditions very bad. First off the Canadians in the trenches get battered by the German artillery, as we fire back. A week later and the Canadians make their move as we fire over the lines, and at last Vimy falls. Everyone is jubilant. We get to meet some of the Canadians. They joke we can't speak English. One of them left the East End with his family for a better life. Can't blame him. But, I think, with no Empire there'd be no need for him to be here risking his life.

At least for now we can take a drink, a smoke, and a rest. I go and rub down the horses.

29 April 1917. One shell burst in the centre of the train causing heavy casualties. Two men were killed outright, two wounded and died soon afterwards and eight others all more or less seriously wounded. Ten horses were killed, one wounded and one missing. All animals that have died since arrival were very weak and deaths were caused by exposure.

I found him in a hollow, blood and mud all over. Dead. No, a twitch. I ran and knelt at his side. He signalled to lean closer to hear. Croaking faint voice.

"Yates. Fred. I want you to have this." He tried to point at it with his missing right hand. A watch.

"I can't. They'll think I stole it from … a dying man. I can't wear an officer's watch."

"Keep it, and remember me. The empire dies with me. Yours is the future. If Oslo …" He died.

Gunner Saddler Yates   47

I sat down, held the watch, looked at it. I flipped open the case. I wept and wept, the first and only time in my life. On the dial was written Wilson and Gill, 139–141 Regents Street, London W1.

The Animals in War Memorial, Brook Gate, Park Lane, London W1, bears the simple testament:

They had no choice

"Nor us," whispers Fred, swirling the leaves.

I stand and reflect on Gunner Sadler Yates, the grandfather I never knew. A man who fought for social change. A man who fought against tyranny. A man whose skills let him make life a little better for horse and man. I feel proud.

Raketa (Rocket) Kopernik, USSR, 1980s, stainless steel, mechanical movement. These watches commemorate the discovery by Copernicus that the earth orbits the sun. The golden disk represents the sun and the hours. The silver circle which revolves around it represents the earth and the minutes. The sweep second hand is conventional.

The Tranquillity of Copernicus

Dreams. The Copernicus sets one off in me that night. The Russian Raketa Copernicus has a clever dial to commemorate the orbital discoveries of the great man. Clever in this case also equates hard to read, especially at dusk. That evening my crepuscular client finds my squinting ers and ahs about whether it's time to finish amusing.

"I won't wear it again," I say, a little defensively.

The nocturne begins. My life here is unmarked by change, I have tranquillity. I was unbegun, now ageless. At least it's not damp, and corpulence feels, feels less pressing. Here I remain trapped in endless looping time, banished by the Royal Court for theft and conspiracy to murder, to spend an eternity looking at life ungraspable. I am denied even death. Worse, worse torture to a watchmaker, I have no solution to a puzzle, set by the genius Breguet.

I sigh at the earth entering my view: blue of sea, striations of clouds, desert coverlets, ripplings of mountains. The moss blanket of forest. All, from this distance, a silent unpeopled heavenly body. Once I look at the sun, turning swiftly from its implacable glare. My ultimate source of being, yes, but one I cannot look upon. Something from the upper world says if I can see the sun I will become the sulphurous black smudge of a spent match.

I'm why I'm here. It wasn't just because of the planned murder, but what I stole. Ending M. Breguet's life would have ended mine at tumbril ride's end. At least I hadn't stopped his grandiloquent project, the commission from Marie Antoinette. No, he stopped it by dying, his greatest unfinished symphony in chronology, to pass to his son. My glorious career was as yet unhatched.

The watch was a commission for the queen in 1783 by a mysterious man known to us all as Count Axel von Fersen. He required of Breguet, supreme watchmaker in Paris, the most fantastic and complicated watch ever for the queen. She collected Breguet watches and shared her bed with von Fersen, admiring both together.

The watch was not completed until 1827, by which time the queen had progressed from *soi-disant* fountainhead to scarlet-headed fountain. As a subject of her boasting the watch had never been a secret. I sought out secrecy.

It wasn't the queen's watch that I desired. Even I knew that an attempt to steal it would have been fatal.

Circumstances had led me to notice M. Breguet had another peculiar watch my hands itched to touch and explore. I, M. Malheureux, who had yet to do anything. So I thought, if I could decipher the operations of this watch I might make my own *Montre du Système Solaire* with unimagined complications. Think, a watch that would show all the planets' motion.

But I get ahead of myself. How did I manage contact with Breguet? I had found my way from Normandy to Paris some years before, a

The Tranquillity of Copernicus   51

boy-man of twenty-one. I knew I had talent, but my father could never further it. Mother made sure I knew this before disappearing with a younger, landed man. As mother said, "You can care for your ailing father, or you can live. I've chosen. Goodbye."

My mother was a witch. The only satisfaction for me was that her lover had a definite preference for me when it came to fleshly pleasures. Oh, the look of longing as he realised he wouldn't be coming back. Still, I had a new more handsome beau, so I cared little.

Father was a watchmaker, but not one of much account, and some of his customers had begun to travel further afield to find someone less likely to crack enamel. I knew the people linked his luckless name with his occupational hazard of a worsening tremor. When someone asked how M. Malheureux was, the answer was always "comme d'habitude" with a wink. One idiot answered "comme il faut" and got a good kicking for his bad French.

Within a few years I became one of the finer watchmakers in Paris, and my name was taken as magically ironic. I was begun at last. The day came when I was accepted to work with Breguet, marking me out in the glory of the finest watchmakers. My great efforts were about to reach fruition. But I had no intention of doing this unaided by Breguet's brain. I had not seen it, but I'd heard whispers about the watch that represented the planets. This man was monstrously and unfairly gifted.

I was trusted with a key so I could get into the workshop, and the men who guarded the premises knew who I was. One night in November I returned after dark saying I had left my spectacles, joking I was lucky I hadn't gone to the wrong address.

I knew which drawer the watch would be in, since Breguet always kept it locked. I wrenched it open carefully, with a cloth thrown over to limit the sound of splitting wood. There were three watches there. One was from the revolutionary period, with the dial divided into ten decimal hours as well as the conventional twelve. An echo from without. "Why did it never catch on?" The second had a completely bare dial. A mystery dial, more than usually cryptic. It appeared a perfect disk of porcelain, with Masonic symbols. The third watch was what I sought. A golden orb marked the trajectory of the sun, surrounded by a thin circle of silver – I presumed the earth. But what showed the seconds? I picked up the key and wound the watch. A very small, perfect silver ball was rolling around the outer track of the dial, once per minute. And there was evidence of something unbelievable. A track in which an object must move in an ellipse. Outside the orbit of the sun? I needed time, light and seclusion to think through all this. As I turned to leave a group of armed men rushed me and pinned me to the floor.

This wasn't the dream I had wanted. M. Breguet was still alive and I had yet to unlock the mysteries of his Copernicus watch (that was my name for it: I could take credit for something). There must have been some very deep-seated envy for me, a watchmaker and collector, to want to murder Brequet as well as steal his secret watch. No more secrets would be his. Oh, and I know, had he lived a shorter time, he'd have made fewer watches, driving up the value of each, and, I thought, making me a billionaire. I wasn't a madman, you see.

My trial was very brief as I was the only suspect, had been witnessed entering the building, and was putting the watch in my specially

The Tranquillity of Copernicus   53

prepared fob when arrested, spectacles on nose. The judge said that the punishment must fit the crime. As I had been trying to steal M. Breguet's planetary secrets, I would be banished there for eternity, to contemplate my folly.

Here I sit on a grey beach with no sea, no gulls, just suspension. Grey beach of ashes to the horizon. I notice I'm sitting on something hard. Surely there are no rocks here? I shift around then put a hand in my pocket. It's still there, they never took it back. Breguet's watch. A shock thrills through me.

There's even a small knife in the other pocket, meant by me to disembowel the horologist. The watch is here, demonstrating its skill. They made sure I had no tools on me so it puzzles me to damnation. I pull the knife out to open the watch case. Before my eyes the blade melts to a stream and drips of mercury.

Black in black. What is this? The earth has gone behind, and soon the sun. I miss the beach. I sit clenching. Teeth, buttocks, hands. Now some pinpricks of stars come if I don't keep my eyes fixed on them. My left hand aches. I open it. There is Breguet's watch. I almost throw it into the inky stillness but a faint glow catches my eye. Points on the dial are beginning to illuminate – sun, earth, and now moon. I can see into the movement; see how these three are connected. An arc of light spreads across me. No! The watch disappears in the brilliance. I blink. It is morning. I am looking at my Soviet Raketa Copernicus with its innocent second hand. Named by the USSR. I'm a nothing again. Fuckerama. Oh, I'd forgotten, I'm not a watchmaker after all.

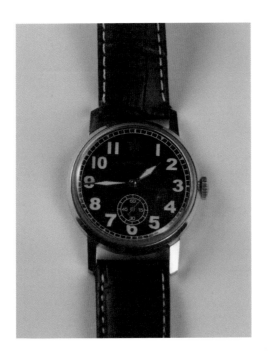

***Pobeda (Victory) SMERSH (a portmanteau for
"Death to Spies" coined by Stalin, or, according to
Wikipedia, an acronym meaning "Special Methods
of Spy Detection. Stalin didn't mince words).***
Stainless steel, 1980s, USSR, mechanical movement.
Various makes and models of Soviet watch celebrate
James Bond's nemesis.

55

Death to Spies

Abstinence

Monday morning. The circle of the abstinence group shift unsurely in their seats. Alice left last week, after completing twelve weeks. A certificate for her and cakes for all. She was well liked, brutally honest and brutally kind. She spared no one, least of all herself.

We were to welcome Robert today. Whoever and however he was, he had to fill an Alice-shaped emotional hole. I had reached the halfway point and knew this always happened when someone left or joined. The leaver was mourned, and the newcomer was on probation. One or two leavers weren't mourned, but their leaving came from a crisis the group couldn't contain. Denying having a problem with alcohol was one, since it isolated the person while angering the rest of us. You don't get referred to drug and alcohol services for nothing. As time passed I learned to make as few assumptions as possible. The "black lesbian" came out when comfortable enough in the group as being a straight woman who had stabbed her partner to death in the street. Convicted of manslaughter, she was out on licence. Her leaving the group was the saddest occasion. It all got too much for her, she drank, and thereby broke her licence conditions.

Frank is taking the group today. He comes in with Robert, on crutches and looking gaunt, the stigmata of many years' drinking on his face. Frank gets us to introduce ourselves to Robert, who is asked for a few words about himself. He is, or was, a sculptor. He is also from a more privileged background than the rest of us. Alcohol really is an equal opportunities drug.

"I'd like us to play a game as an icebreaker," says Frank. "I'd like you each to say two things about yourself. One of them should be true, the other one a lie. Then the rest of us have to guess which is true."

It comes to my turn. I've played this game before and I'm always interested in the result.

"I have a degree in philosophy; and many years ago I was interviewed by MI6 to be a spy."

Everyone except Robert gets the wrong answer.

I ask Robert how he came to the correct conclusion. "I don't know you yet, but the philosophy degree would sit easily with how you seem to me. Being a spy would be outrageous. So it was a bluff. Mind you, if you ever signed the Official Secrets Act we'll never know whether we can trust you.

With a mixture of humour and great discomfort, I reply, "No, you won't."

Intelligence

Death to Spies   57

Twenty years earlier. I'm preparing for my Master's degree exams in anthropology, at the School of Colonial and Commonwealth Studies. I'm hoping to go on to be an academic, but this will depend on success now and a PhD later. I wonder what else I could do with my life and conclude, like many others, that there's always the Civil Service. There's a fast track graduate recruitment scheme involving a set of IQ-style tests followed by interviews for the fortunate.

I go for the IQ-style exam, knowing my numeracy isn't great. Anything I learn about numbers or statistics has a short half-life in my brain.

I sit nervously at the beginning of a ritual I've endured every year since I was eleven. The desks set out with military precision. The wall clock. The "You may turn your papers over now and begin. You have three hours." The peregrinating invigilator with paper supplies. I don't know at this point it will be the last time I have to do this, except for my MA exams.

By exam end I'm reasonably confident I've failed. I didn't like doing any of it, not only the numbers. As I expect I receive a letter marked On Her Majesty's Service a week later stating that I have failed, together with my marks. To my surprise I passed well in the literacy section, and failed fairly narrowly in numeracy. As with membership of Royal Colleges of Medicine exams, you have to pass both sections at the same time; you cannot carry forward a partial pass. So I've failed. So service of my country goes on the rubbish heap. I'm not interested in coming back and trying again.

A week later there's a surprise for me. There's a letter in a manila envelope with no OHMS on it. I'm surprised when I open it to find it seems to be from the Foreign Office, although it doesn't exactly say that. It doesn't exactly say much. It opens by acknowledging that I have recently sat the exams for the civil service graduate recruitment scheme. It makes no reference to my failure, but says that they have other jobs I might be interested in, and a phone number to contact about a first interview. I have a friend I knew in Oxford who is now studying Arabic at SCCS, funded by the Foreign Office. I have a suspicion about what all of this is, but I know he will be able to tell me. The last sentence of the letter reads "You will notice that this letter is addressed to you personally and confidentially, and we hope you will respect this confidence." Had I wished to work in the intelligence services I might have paid attention.

My friend Jonathan from the Foreign Office immediately confirms that I will be interviewed by MI6. My objection that my exam performance shows I'm not intelligent enough is brushed aside by Jonathan. "They will be interested in you chiefly because you were at Oxford and now at SCCS. SCCS was founded as a think tank on the colonies. After Oxbridge they are the biggest recruitment ground for spooks. A senior member of staff here has been identified as the recruiting link. It's better if I don't tell you who he is."

"I'm about as patriotic as a baguette, but I really can't resist the temptation of going to a first interview, then pulling out. My worry is whether I would be made to sign the Official Secrets Act before interview."

"I can't answer that for sure. They probably wouldn't for an initial interview, and if that's the case they won't tell you what job you're

Death to Spies   59

applying for. If they do they'll tell you that's what you are signing and you can run away then. Come and let me know what happens afterwards."

The week before the interview is filled with ruminations which convince me I must not go forward beyond a first interview, no matter what might be on offer. After signing the Official Secrets Act I realise I will be condemned to a double life. I will not be able to discuss my working day, even with a partner. And given any partner will be male, I will be doubly damned. I will have to hide any sexual relationship from my employers because in the 1980s homosexuality is seen as a security risk.

The interview is in Carlton House Terrace, a row of Classical stuccoed villas by John Nash, right at the heart of Establishment London. I ring the doorbell. A woman in her thirties, smartly dressed, lets me in.

"Mr Forsythe?"

"Yes."

"I'm Miss Millington. I'll just sign you in." She goes into an anteroom and produces a register. I'm looking for words like 'This seals your fate', but there's nothing, so I sign.

"You're seeing Mr Summersly."

"Yes, that's what it says in the letter of invitation."

"Please take a seat over there and I'll take you to his office shortly."

"Thank you."

It's beginning to feel a bit strange. Miss Millington was all brisk friendly attention. The building has red carpeting throughout. Long corridors and wide stairways. Oak doors and polished brass knobs. There is absolutely no sign of life. Not even a single sound of human converse. I'm left in this mausoleum for about fifteen minutes, then Miss Millington appears and takes me to the interview.

"Ah, come in, Mr Forsythe. Please come in and take a seat." There is only one, on the other side of the large desk from Mr Summersly. It's a large office. I have the gnawing thought that Hitler had something like this designed by Speer for the Reich Chancellery. So he could easily intimidate visitors. Not that he needed a big desk for that.

"You may be wondering why you're here?"

"Well yes, I am. As I failed the graduate entry tests in particular."

"According to the information we have you did very well on verbal reasoning and only just failed on the maths. That needn't be a blanket objection. In fact we find verbal ability is probably more important in

Death to Spies   61

our area of work.

"When you were a student in Oxford, did you make contact with people with whom you remain in contact?"

"Yes, I've kept a number of friends, most of whom also moved to London."

"Would you describe any of these as useful contacts?"

"Useful?"

"Well, for example, in positions of influence?"

"Ah, it happens an old friend is now also at SCCS too. He's in the Foreign Office, and we do discuss some matters to do with the current government."

"Good. I think his name is Jonathan?"

"Yes, it is." Again, that slightly uneasy feeling.

"In your last year at Oxford you visited the Indian Department of Forestry in Simla, Himachal Pradesh. Would you say you made useful contacts there?"

"Well, I met some very informative people. It was helpful to me as I was completing my degree in agricultural science and forestry. They've called it Shimla since independence." When I start to get bored and frustrated my mouth behaves like this.

"Well observed, Mr Forsythe"

The interview continues in similar vein. I know he is trying to ascertain how good I might be at extracting information from someone, short of torturing them (I hope). What makes it seem ridiculous to me is that what's on the menu at the Foreign Office canteen on a particular week, or which kind of pine is most productive at an altitude of 8,000 feet in Himachal Pradesh doesn't seem militarily useful.

At last we get to my opportunity to ask questions. The first is the most obvious.

"You've mentioned you may have several jobs relevant to me, but the problem is that I don't know what these are. In fact, I don't know any more than I did before the interview."

"The trouble is that these jobs come up periodically and in different departments so I'd have to wait to see what's there."

"Is this the first of a series of interviews, assuming you are interested in

Death to Spies   63

me?"

"Again, I can't really say."

I know for sure now that I have not signed the Official Secrets Act. Now I can make my proscenium arch speech.

"This has been an unusual experience for me. I've never heard before of someone being recruited for a job when nothing is said about what the job is. Having enquired of others, I have reason to believe that this is about recruitment to the Intelligence Services. If that is the case, I must say now that I have no interest whatsoever in working for MI6."

"I'm afraid I can't comment on that."

Within a week the letter came stating that no jobs had been identified for which I was suitable at the moment.

Over coffee I discussed the experience with Jonathan. He smiled throughout. Things were weirder than I'd already concluded.

"So, Mr Summersly, what was he like?"

"Not noteworthy. Probably in his fifties, medium height, balding. He wore specs."

"The Mr Summersly who interviewed me was about thirty-five, over six feet tall, no specs."

"Do you mean that even for an interview at which the Official Secrets Act hasn't been signed they use false identities?"

"It seems so. They could even do it in drag, but I don't think they've ever gone that far, except in a more adventurous honey trap."

"I was just thinking, if I'd done really really appallingly badly in the exam, perhaps I could have gone on to be head of the service."

A few days later I'm wandering absentmindedly over Waterloo Bridge. I pause to watch the river traffic. A stiff-looking besuited man hits me a little too hard with his umbrella.

"You're in the way."

I'm about to call out something genital when I freeze. Georgi Markov, dissident Bulgarian, killed by a ball of ricin inflicted with an umbrella on Waterloo Bridge. Just because I'm paranoid doesn't mean I'm wrong.

Abstinence again

Death to Spies

Robert really has come very close to death. He says this is his last chance to quit alcohol. In the weeks that follow I come to like this man very much. He brings in something he has sculpted. A hare in dark wood, ready to spring forward. He says it has been years since he has felt the urge to create. Now it is enveloping him. He doesn't look well, but his spirit is alive. He brings warmth to the group.

It comes time for me to leave the group and find my own way. I am happier and healthier, more secure.

The next year I relapse. During a severe episode of depression I drink when I learn my mother has died. This time I'm admitted with alcoholic hepatitis for a week's inpatient detox.

I'm dry. I'm allowed to return to the abstinence group.

It's with considerable relief I arrive at the familiar building and enter the room. I introduce myself. It's good to know already that this meeting may be difficult as I'm the new person. It's just how it will be difficult I don't imagine.

Frank comes in.

"Hello … Welcome back."

"I'm happy to be back. I hope I won't be back again."

"Oh … I thought I'd better tell you, as you were the only one in the group then. I had a call last week. Robert died a month ago."

I'm stunned. I begin to shake, my eyes glisten.

"It turned out it was too late for him. He had multiple organ failure, after he started to drink again."

At first I think, sometimes it really is too late. During the session I am distracted, thinking mainly of Robert. In the end I can smile. He really had come alive again when I last saw him. However little time there is, it is always worth living intensely, now.

Poljot (Flight) alarm watch, gold tone, 1980s, USSR, mechanical movement. This watch has a radial dial. Instead of the numerals remaining upright they follow the radial progress of the hands. Conventionally, with Arabic numerals 4-8 revert to being the right way up to avoid 6 being completely inverted. This dial is rare in having the rotation consistent right round the dial. With Roman numeral radial dials it is the other way round, the usual arrangement being to have VI inverted.

Flight

Dad holds my hand. I look up at the bulbous nose, motherly, inviting. She has a friendly face. She points at the sky invitingly. Come aboard. Then a tremendous roar starts ever so slowly, reaching a crescendo which terrifies my four-year-old self. Propellers spin ever more wildly and the beast starts to move. Now male, voracious, predatory. The grass billows as the monster begins to turn. I remember no more, neither the taxi nor the take-off. What remains? The glimmer of silver and green on a summer day. The morphing of slumbering whale into teeth-baring shark.

Since then, whenever I see a Douglas DC3, something moves in my unconscious. The plane links me to my father. He calls it a Dakota, the name adopted in Britain during World War 2. I love this name. Like a faithful dog or contented cat. It is the plane at rest, not the monster. It is with me through my life. Come aboard.

Years pass. The number of these machines dwindles. I accept crumbs from the table; turn my head skywards whenever I hear those engines; see them in film, even in the unlikely hands of James Bond in a subterranean lakeland.

Years later I learn of the Berlin Airlift, the first big standoff of the Cold War. Valiant armies of military DC3s and other craft bearing fuel, goods and food to the West Berliners. The Soviets back off in 1949 after nearly a year of land blockade. Berlin has not been starved into submission.

Flight

There is a little story everyone knows. The children gather at Tempelhof Airport to watch and cheer, or in the streets where they live. Someone has the idea of dropping sweets to them. Soon small parachutes descend bearing chocolate, gum, and other goodies. They call the planes *Rosinenbomber*, Candy Bomber. How strange, I think, that post-war German children should use the term bomber. Perhaps not. The only gifts from the skies they have known have devastated them. The planes must have been perceived as their feminine selves. I read a little more and find the answer. The pilot who began this habit, the USAF's Gail Halvorsen, became known as the Candy Bomber by his colleagues. As well as dropping sweets he wiggled his wings to show the children it was him.

During the noughties I visit Berlin for the first time. Just to begin with I don't like it. Too spread out; too much demolition work; no discernible heart or centre. And the drains smell (in Germany?). But as the capital of unified Germany develops, like a phoenix, I like it more and more.

I pick up a leaflet one day in 2007 in my guesthouse in Moabit. Nostalgia flights from Tempelhof Airport in a genuine Rosinenbomber military Douglas C-47. My interest is grabbed, and how much, I think, Dad would have liked this. The plane was built in 1944 and converted for military use before ferrying troops from England to the liberation of Europe during early 1945. Since then, she had had many guises, but was properly made a flying museum in 2000. Of course, the following two years would be the sixtieth anniversary of the Berlin Airlift, and a poignant time to go aboard, or so I hoped.

I returned to Berlin the following year, but somehow booking the flight didn't fit with my other plans. Ah well, I can still go next year and be

70   Watchwords

part of the sixtieth anniversary. Then comes a first disappointment. Tempelhof Airport is to be closed for redevelopment at the end of October 2008, in spite of campaigns to keep it in use as an airfield. I won't be able to fly from Tempelhof in 2009. A pity. The airport had served the city since 1930, so was not tainted by Hitler other than by his use of it. Its long, modernist terminal building was justly famous. And of course it was where the Berlin Airlift happened.

My immediate worry after the disappointment is whether the flights will be happening at all. Relief as I go online. For 2009 the flights will be based at Schönefeld, Berlin's chosen main airport for the forthcoming years. I click and pay for a flight in July 2009. For my €150 (up from last year, I note) I get a champagne reception at the terminal, a documentary about the Airlift, and a half-hour flight on the plane over Berlin's famous landmarks. Anticipatory glee makes me smile.

My 2009 visit is with my friend Stephen. We're interested this time in more recent Berlin history, pre- to post-war. The 1936 Olympic Stadium, the Haus der Wannsee Conferenz and the Stasi Museum are all on our list, as is the Liebeskind-designed Holocaust Museum.

Stephen does not like flying. I haven't tried to force him onto the Candy Bomber as the flight is something very personal to me. But I point out that the aircraft was part of one of Berlin's greatest events of the previous century.

"Only just," he says sardonically. "I don't want to get on anything which looks like it's missing a tail gunner."

Flight   71

"Oh, that's just silly. I think you need some CBT for flight anxiety. Not from me."

A year later he will wave a newspaper article in my face which shocks and deeply saddens me at the same time. Eleven months after my flight the Candy Bomber will crash.

No one is seriously hurt, but the plane is badly damaged. It feels like a bereavement.

"I wasn't so silly after all," says Stephen, all reasonable. There's nothing I can say to him. I'm hurting too much.

In Berlin

The good of being anally punctual is always being early. The bad is always being early. Being anally punctual usually depends on anxiety, thus the relief of arriving safely is offset by the sense of a wasted life until the thing you've arrived for happens. Being habitually late can be due to anxiety too, or stupidity, or an underdeveloped worriability, not in itself unattractive. Being either early or late can have a number of other influences of interest only to therapists and pedants. Being habitually on time is a mystery, or involves deceptions such as walking round the block or reverse time travel.

I arrived at Flughaufen Schönefeld two hours early. I looked around for what I expected to be either an art deco or workmanlike building.

Then I noticed that "Candy Bomber" next to the main airport terminal was not in fact a sweet shop. Somehow the obvious title did not connect in my brain with the purpose of the building. I say building. Large Portakabin. It looked like something the Chinese had made – a basic model on which to append whatever was suitable, to make, just possibly, a rock-bottom-price terminal for a dangerous airline, an American diner, or a sweet shop. American diner was what stuck in my mind as I walked through doors which looked chrome deco but were automatic.

Somebody had paid attention to period detail. All the staff were in uniform, correct for the late 1940s. With uniforms you either don't like them or, if you do, you like them to be worn properly. The problem here was that the staff appeared to be a burlesque troupe picking up a bit of daytime work. A very camp burlesque troop. It's highly unlikely there was a heterosexual man in the ground staff. The women looked like they'd seen it all before, darling.

I went to the check-in desk.

"Could I see your passport, sir, please?" Big wink.

"My passport? Why would I need that? We're only going to fly round Berlin at a few thousand metres. We're not leaving the country."

"But you have to have your passport. You will be entering international airspace."

Flight   73

"No we aren't, that's at one thousand kilometres above the earth." Smug me as usual.

"Technically, sir, you are leaving the European Union, so you need your passport." A prescient comment, as you will realise. "I am sorry, but you will not be allowed to board the flight."

"But nobody told me about this."

"It was in the information pack we sent you, in bold."

I had to admit it to myself; like a lot of tedious rubbish (my description), I had not bothered to read this. I wanted to punch the pouting man in uniform now, but then one of the women introduced herself and said, "Do you have your driving licence with you? That might be enough to identify you."

Bless you for ever, whatever your name was.

After a brief hushed discussion behind the check-in they decide to let me board using my driving licence. I was going to suggest they could have made up fun 1940s passports in bright colours, pink, yellow, orange, for us to fill in ourselves, but decide it's not the right moment.

I think I'm done.

"Sir, you aren't on the passenger list." It's Mr Mimsy again.

"What?"

"You aren't on the passenger list for 10.30."

"That's because I'm booked for 12.30."

"So why are you here now?"

"I'm early." At this point I want to do several unspeakable things to Mr Mimsy.

"Well, you will have to wait for two hours. Outside the building, as there is no seating here, and you are not allowed into the reception room until precisely 12.30."

At this point, my guardian angel looks up from a piece of paper.

"Look, Wolf, someone was delayed for 10.30. Mr Neal could take his place, then at 12.30 the delayed party will be here. Everyone's happy."

Flight   75

Wolf doesn't look convinced, but allows the arrangement. Flexible Germans. Good. Pleasantly unexpected.

There is one extra problem. It is now 11.00, which means I have messed up the programme. The plan to fit me in early will only work if I do the video first, then the flight, and finally the reception. This is of no significance to me. I can see, though, it upsets Wolf's sense of *ordnung* and *comme il faut*.

The other guests are now milling through from the reception to the screening room. I'm handed an audio guide. The sound track for the documentary is in German. The "Candy Bomber Experience" has been pushed as an international experience. The ground staff have all spoken English fluently until now. The first thing which doesn't is the audio guide. Completely refuses to work. I let myself imagine the voiceover is just descriptive, not straining its audience with metaphor. One of the German fathers is laughing and picking his nose, so I think I'm right.

Film over, we pass through a short corridor and are let out onto the tarmac. There she is, nose proudly in the sky. Silver, "Rosinenbomber" elegantly scripted along her flank. She is about 200 metres away. This is an airport, so we cannot walk to her, as I would like to have done, to be introduced. The bus picks us up and puts us down a minute later. A new woman, looking perfectly 1940s demure, is standing in the doorway, our air hostess. If I'd been organising this, it would have been cocktails in flight, not a terrestrial reception, but I reserve judgement. We are told we will be commencing the flight shortly, but there will be plenty of time for pictures and questions when we land.

Up a short flight of steps and into the belly of the graceful whale. The most friendly, lovely whale I have seen is a beluga, at Vancouver Aquarium, so I decide she's one of these. There's no baggage hold, so we are standing in an oval tube. There are only twenty-five seats, but this means we have plenty of room to stretch out. I am in a single seat behind the port engine. As the nose of the plane tilts uphill you feel something is about to happen as soon as you're in your seat.

The captain will be coming to address us about our trip. I am dripping with anticipation. There must be some special reason for keeping him out of sight until now. I think swooning maidens, gay men, all the war films I've ever seen, but it's not about the uniform, I reassure myself. It certainly isn't. Our captain is called Heinrich. He's the sort of man you wouldn't want approaching you in a bar. He looks like a ferret, and possibly smells like one too. Same uniform as the others, but a captain's cap which doesn't match, and aviator shades. He puts one foot on a box, parks his chewing gum in one cheek, and starts talking in an accent which even I know is not the German equivalent of David Niven. I really, really hope this man is acting. I hope even more that the person who has scripted him is dead. You've ruined the fantasy of a little boy. If only I'd read a book on how to hijack a plane. I could have had flying lessons too. I wonder what the co-pilot looks like. Is there one? At least we didn't have to listen to it all again in tortured English from Heinrich.

You see, I have always been the pilot too. Since that first day on the grass at Ipswich Airport. She is mine. I am the candy man. We are part of each other. I will be the smart, swooned-at aviator, the protector in the mother ship. I will save Berlin/anywhere that needs saving. I will bring everyone safe home. And all without a hint of vanity. A lower case messiah. This is why I will cry inwardly when I hear next year that Ursula is hurt. Ursula?

Flight 77

My reverie shuts down. As soon as Heinrich disappears back into the cockpit my fit of self-pity abates. I can contemplate Ursula again, the name I've chosen for my plane.

Now I'm all attention. I mustn't miss any of the next thirty minutes. The starter motor begins to spin the propeller blades outside the window to my left. With a flash of fire the engine bursts into life. Grows louder. I am four again. I expect to be overwhelmed by the noise. No. It's not even very loud. The starboard engine joins in, and we begin to taxi. I feel like the queen in a carriage, processing down the Mall. No, imagine being in the carriage as myself. Myself at four. Myself now. Both are me.

They should have brought along hundreds of people dressed as the poor of Berlin in 1949 to wave us off. Uh, did I say no vanity?

We wait on the runway. The propellers spin ever faster. We wobble a bit, like an athlete on the blocks. Then we are off, not like a jet plane, but still with that rush of energy I always feel on take-off. Plus the odd sensation of the tail wheel rising so we are at last horizontal. Finally a gentle lift and rise into the air, a bank to the left, and we rise to cloud level. It is July, but cloudy. To be able to see the sights we have to stay below the clouds, at about one thousand metres.

I don't need translation. I see the Tiergarten, *terra incognita* on East German maps in 1949. I know there are rabbits beneath the trees and in the glades, as well as the more spectacular residents of the zoological gardens. Then I disconcert myself briefly. Schönefeld, where we just took off, was the airport for East Berlin at the time. This is all bloody wrong and anachronistic. How *could* Berlin have closed

78   Watchwords

Tempelhof and spoiled my experience? How could Germany have allowed it?

Then the Olympic Stadium, which I have seen at ground level, hoves into view, spectacular, free of all Nazi identifiers. They've scrubbed Hitler off the commemoration plaque. It's obvious he once filled the hole in the middle. The bell tower no longer stands, but the huge bronze bell is on the ground. This was subject to a compromise. Rubbing off bronze swastikas several centimetres thick is no mean task, so they rubbed off arms here and there to leave no complete manifestation of the worst symbol the world has known.

For a moment I imagine I am Vivien Leigh, smiling out of a DC3 window at Manhattan's 1939 skyline. Then I remember some of her affliction has been mine (though not the beauty and delicacy) and I notice another familiar feeling begin to descend. Already, by the age of four, I had developed the euphemistically titled malady of motion discomfort. This better suits constipation in our less euphemistic British English. I don't know what I called it at the time, but now it's nausea and vomiting, starting as car sickness. I would rather eat a sheep's testicles than go on a cruise across the Atlantic or the rides on a funfair. I know, because I've eaten them.

What would Vivien Leigh do? This is not a helpful question. I spend the second half of my once in a lifetime flight gripping the arms of my seat, wishing I were anywhere but here. The air hostess comes round, asking us if we'd like her to take pictures of us. Whatever I say through gritted teeth is taken as a yes. Reluctantly I hand her my Nikon and she snaps away. Fortunately for me I'd forgotten to replace the macro lens with the normal one, so my grey and green grave face is erased forever.

Flight

Ruined, ruined, everything is ruined. It's like Claridge's have a dungeon which I've been sent to for the rest of my stay. These are a few of my least favourite things: nausea, kidney stones, and depression. A valiant attempt at positive thinking, which I don't believe in. This is all the fault of the Heinrich the *il s'abuse pour il s'amuse* pilot for throwing the plane round like a bad bus driver. Nothing to do with the weather.

We bank rather alarmingly for the final approach to the runway and a heave from my lower regions nearly douses the other British passengers in front of me with bile. I can only think thank goodness I didn't have the reception first.

Deep breaths, deep breaths. Within a few minutes I'm feeling better. Of course I'd known that there's much more turbulence at low altitude. That's why we have pressurised cabins now and fly above ten thousand metres. In the Dakota it was a bit like bumping along in a Land Rover, only you can't see where the bumps are so you can't prepare yourself. My body has never liked surprises; adolescence; waking up. I was cheery again by the time I took my photos, and asked someone to take a picture of me, holding fondly onto one of Ursula's propeller blades. On the ground she was entirely beneficent and to my liking. Of course, I also thought that being her pilot was an even more unlikely fantasy now than I had before.

We caught the bus back to the terminal shed. I said goodbye to the people I'd almost vomited over. We had a lovely chat, which could have been spoiled. I was sent round the outside of the building as I had to go back through the entrance to get to the reception. All the others were there already, sipping their drinks and nibbling at or stuffing in their doughnuts. Of course there was someone with a list which I wasn't on waiting at the door, and I had several more minutes of fuming before I was allowed to go to the bar.

"Champagne, my dear?" said a very knowing barman. He handed me a small flute of Sekt. A note to the French: you really must enforce your rules, even if you and Germany are the high table of the EU.

"Doughnut?"

It looked as if he'd been sampling these between guest groups for a few months now. I was about to say something about his costumes fitting when he went back to the theatre, when the platter of doughnuts caught my attention. Some were un-iced. Others came in a choice of turquoise, puce or black icing. They were of various sizes and shapes. Curiously, I wanted to eat them. All.

"Are you a ring or a mouthful man?" says the barman.

"That's far too large to fit in my mouth." I do have rather a small mouth.

"You prefer the ring, then?"

I don't know whether I want to punch him or fuck him so I burst out laughing.

Flight

After getting home from Berlin I look through a collection of my father's photographs and colour slides. Among the latter are a couple of frames from that long-ago summer day at Ipswich Airport. There's my first Ursula. We are some way off from her. There's a line of people waiting patiently to board. It's a small airline flying to the Channel Islands.

Once the passengers had boarded we must have moved closer. My memory was of being almost under the plane, but memory is unreliable, and to a small child everything is bigger. Whichever, regulations were laxer in those days. I knew after seeing Ursula number two in Berlin that even if we had been standing right under the engines we wouldn't have been decapitated. Well, Dad might, I'll have to look at the photo of me holding Ursula number two's propeller again.

To the child all is big, new, astonishing the first time. Later, mundane, prone to disappoint. Wonder becomes dismay if we don't act on our world.

Entering experience is different from regarding it. The looking engages imagination. I saw a gentle mother and a fearsome beast. I dreamed of a handsome rescuing hero, and of me being that hero. I saw the Dakota as comfort and attraction. It did a very good thing in the bleak days of 1948–1949. It will always be with me. And it is a connection to dad and his love of planes, from his boyhood witnessing of the Battle of Britain at Biggin Hill.

As soon as I was on the ground, Ursula Two was my friend of fantasy again. When I later heard she had crashed I felt wrenched. My relief is that she is so important to history that she is to be restored and fly once again.

My sympathy goes out to all of you who get "motion discomfort" of stomach or lower regions. I'm fine in cars as an adult, but I can't sit backwards on a bus. A log flume is enough to make me scream, then feel embarrassed when I look back and see how small it was. It's the falling sensation. Perhaps Ursula Two felt sick when she fell from the sky?

The experience of a lifetime disappointed on many levels. Material reality. No matter, the dream remains. At least nausea ends when you vomit.

Ursula means little bear. So the Dakota was a little bear and a beluga whale. Ursula was my mother's middle name.

Flight

Contemporary watch produced in China for the British Museum, stainless steel, quartz movement. The dial bears modern Arabic numerals as found on watches made for the Middle East and South Asia.

Our Song is Love Unknown

In our beautiful mountain city we were children when men first chose war to encompass us. Do you remember our first separation, Habibti? Hope and terror in the air. Could it be that Saddam, always felt, sometimes seen, could be erased from our lives?

Do you remember our walks into the mountains beyond Ranya, above the lake? Pure air, snow-fingered mountains. The forest, the olive-groved villages, the high bleak grassland where we fell, held each other, picnicked. Our Kurdistan, we thought. Briefly, that winter of 1991, we felt the strangler's hands of Saddam might be gone.

I remember how it started. Two small schoolgirls, running, playing, giggling. You loved to be tickled; I hated it. Our school fell apart. No books, no fresh water, but we survived. Boys were foreign to us in many ways, foreign until our demanded marriages. But as girls that was all to come and out of mind. Then the uprising. My father had to flee to Baghdad while you stayed in Ranya. I was bereft. Then I knew that I loved you.

It took another war to reunite us. The explosions in the midnight air and scream of jets. This was terror immediate and daily. My brain couldn't stop long enough to think of Saddam this time. What I didn't know was that it was not a missile which would destroy my life. At last the message came that you were in the city with your family.

Now a new terror. Daesh. They declare death on the gays. You don't need to be there to see. A phone is enough. Men beheaded, men hanged, men pushed from buildings. We quiver in fear. The niqab is our friend. Men. They don't believe in women's being except in subordination. Sex is male. How could a woman do such a thing to another?

Ten seconds only needed to hatch a betrayal. We are like sisters, but sisters don't touch each other like that; make noises like that. My baby brother goes to my father and asks him, "What are they doing?" Family dishonour. We left.

I hide, I survive. I reside now in myself, and I want not to be hidden. Of course, being a lesbian in Iraq was filled with danger. But if they had never known? We two in our niqabs, moving through the souk. Our eyes smiling at each other. A careful stroke of the hand, a whispered "my love". Baghdad. Was it so difficult to hide there?

Now I am in London. I can be as I like, appear in whatever clothes, no need to hide. The niqab hid me, but it was no chosen disguise. It hid what would be abominable. The abomination sits here in plain view. I am butch. A butch lesbian, I am called. I am also confused with myself. Is this "identity" female, male, or both? What creature am I? These women here, these liberated lesbians, they are like men. They are for ever seducing and moving on. Rootless, like trees scudding away, torn up in a storm. I want to be married, to live in a family, belong to a community. Dedicate myself to my wife and children.

You see, I thought England would be a paradise, where all are accepted as they are. It is so much pain that this is not true. I have a master's degree from Baghdad. Yes, I have my refugee status now. At least the

Home Office didn't doubt I am a lesbian, with my jeans and short hair and masculine manner. Still I must search out menial jobs. I like the ones done by men. I would be a security guard, and went for selection. They made it clear I wasn't one of them. I was a dyke.

No one spoke up for me. I knew it was pointless to inform the employers as I wasn't employed yet by them. You have to be from the right part of society, already be part of the new order, before the fruits of Great British progress fall in your orchard.

This you won't believe. I moved to Stamford Hill, the area of London where the Hasidic Jews live. You may think how could I possibly be more different from them. I watched them chatting in the street, with their buggies and cheerful children. They belonged to each other first, then to London, a city of flight. I wanted to so much to belong to a community such as theirs. I longed, I pined, for a Hasidic woman as my wife. One more thing I will never have.

Habibti, I know your father ordered your death.

Our Song is Love Unknown   87

Hamilton Odysee 2001, automatic movement, stainless steel, 1968, Swiss made for US watch company. The Odysee was made to coincide with the release of Stanley Kubrick's film 2001: a Space Odyssey, in 1968. The odd spelling of Odyssey was due to a dispute over copyright between Kubrick and Hamilton.

Strange Odyssey

Paranoid? Not me, much. What if your brain leaves its moorings but you don't know? Floats on an Odyssey without your permission?

This all begins on Facebook. Something's appeared on my timeline on 16 November. Disturbing. Monstrous even. This is not fiction.

> "We shall make you want to squeal Mr Bond, as soon as this Vulcan's flown out of my ear. It's that time of year again. Robin Hood shouldn't and Friar Paul mustn't. Yes, 22 November is our Joint Birthday, conveniently on Monday, so I shall come and have a watch on 27th. On 21st I have to climb two trees (ha ha) as friends of mine have built two of them. I say it's the squirrels."

Fuck. Looks at first glance that only I could have posted it. I would need to be very drunk, and I haven't touched alcohol for two years. A visitation? Can someone have hacked into my account and defecated this stuff there? I scramble for reassurance. My friends, and my sister, say no, you couldn't have written this, it looks like drunken ravings. Then an IT geek says with pride, yes, people can hack into Facebook accounts.

Relief. The content sounds mad. My last port of call is my psychiatrist. No, he doesn't think I'm experiencing psychotic symptoms. On the other hand, he says he has no explanation for my Vulcan and squirrels, so it could be online trolling.

Life continues, nothing unusual. My laptop is giving up on me. I decide to try a Chromebook, recently available. It does everything online, very light, long battery life. I order a small one on Amazon. Too small, it seems. With the ten-inch screen my banana fingers make too many mistakes on the keyboard, so I'll have to consider something bigger. I rebox the ten-inch and send it back to Amazon, asking for substitution of a larger model.

Two days later I open my flat door to find an identical box, left by my neighbour. I think, why have Amazon returned it to me, and within such a short time? I open the box. It's the same Chromebook. They've sent the wrong one. I box it up again then notice something. On the label. It's from the USA. What on earth are they doing? They claim I placed an order on the US website. A second order for something I'd already decided I didn't want.

Now I begin to wonder who is doing this to me. And why? Something similar happened once before. An item from an online catalogue arrived, correctly addressed to me, which I had not ordered. Do I have someone with a grudge against me? Or just a hoaxer or hoaxers? This is nastily novel. I'm leaning towards believing in an imagined enemy. Who is it most likely to be? If (no, because) these events are related, the timescale begins when I worked in the NHS. I can't think of a colleague or client who would hate me. Wait, yes I can. A client whom I had seen for many sessions. I found it very difficult to like him. No, be honest, I didn't like him. Sitting in a room with a narcissist for fifty hours (not consecutive!) isn't fun. He's a man with a very high IQ and one parent with several psychiatric disorders who has been violent. I was still training, and found myself in a trap. The client, Terence (never

Terry) had written an essay about his problems and sent it to me before our first appointment. He listed his emotional problems, then offered his conclusion as to their cause.

He had decided that his impulsive and uncontrollable rages originated with one of his school teachers who had used corporal punishment inappropriately, and frequently. He hated the private education system. He hated his parents for sending him there. His nemesis picked on him because he thought he was gay. In fact he wasn't. Officially sanctioned punishments were done using a cane in the headmaster's office, with a witness present. Mr Copeland preferred to get Terence on his own and use anything to hand. Punishments were always from behind, and Terence strongly suspected that Copeland masturbated at the same time.

At this stage I was very sensitive to my client's account of what had happened to him. It sounded brutal and random. He was thinking of taking Copeland to court. Now retired, Copeland had gone on to a distinguished career as headmaster of a major public school and supporter of worthy causes. Terence didn't want him to die with an untarnished reputation. This was not revenge, it was about making sure Copeland could never do it again.

The longer I worked with Terence, the more I thought Copeland a side track to the major traumas in his life. I'm used to a discrepancy between my intuitions and what a client presents. With Terence, I didn't notice the warnings about how far this would go.

A dream. I am walking near the British Museum on a sunlit afternoon. Comes an apparition, silent and fast, round the corner. It is Terence,

Strange Odyssey

pushing his mother in her wheelchair. She holds a large black knife, not glinting, though her eyes, which are, narrow at me. A Bates? Kathy this time, not Norman's mother.

"You're Neal, aren't you? The therapist who's poisoned my son against me. Don't think I didn't know where he was going. My friend in your department gave me his name."

Terence has turned to clay.

"You should have believed him," she says. "You have no voice to command me."

My throat is solid.

"I am your black knight." With that the raven blade comes forward. I wake on a sudden intake of breath.

A year after I've finished working with Terence I get an email from him. On my birthday. He has decided to go for a prosecution of Copeland, and the police will be contacting me about access to any session notes I have. I'm dumbstruck. My notes aren't evidential. Because my interpretations of Terence's story are at variations with his insistence, he doesn't know my "evidence" could be as useful to the defence as the prosecution. What if I'm called to give evidence, the defence is successful in portraying Terence as a fantasist, and I get to look like an idiot? What if. What if. Paranoia. Marcus is sure I'm paranoid.

A further year passes, I hear nothing, and forget about Terence. A phone call. The police. They have all my computerised notes on Terence from the NHS. I no longer work for the NHS, so the irony is I have no access to those notes myself. They want to see me, don't really say why. An officer visits me at home. The CPS is satisfied there is a case to be made against Copeland. He has been arrested. The trial begins in three weeks. What the officer wants is any handwritten notes I have kept on Terence. I panic. I lie and say I have none. I ask if I'm to be called as a witness. Highly unlikely, but I may be.

I await news with trepidation. The due date for the trial passes. No contact from the authorities. Nothing in the media. My anxiety abates. Back to normal until – it suddenly strikes me, the case may have been abandoned by the judge for lack of evidence. Or contrary evidence. Perhaps my notes have sundered the case? Impulsive anger and rages. What is Terence capable of? He doesn't know where I live. Does he?

Emails return to spook me. I visit Chronology for an opinion on something, and they say they thought my idea was a good one. What idea? The idea to write a set of short stories inspired by my watches.

It is a recent inspiration, but I've told no one yet. How could they know in the shop? It was an email I'd sent the previous night.

At home I look. There really is an email from my account. It's full of errors and things about watches involved in bank robberies and sex

Strange Odyssey　　　93

scandals. These were not among the scenarios I'd envisaged.

Another dream. We have dropped sail travelling on a gulet along the Turkish Aegean coast. It is very quiet, we are drifting, heading into open water. So different from chugging under motor power from one delightful bay to another. With no warning we surge forward, There's no power propelling us. Something fathoms under has grabbed us and is pulling. A great wave covers the prow. The sky blackens, and the water. We are about to die.

In the waking world there is one more mysterious purchase online. Somebody buys me a video product from a psychotherapy organisation, about trauma and dissociation. This is terrifying, as I suspect I'm dissociating, and it cost several hundred pounds. Can it possibly be Terence's revenge?

It's time for my quarterly appointment with my psychiatrist, Dr Scott. I decide it's best to be honest about all of what's happened, even if it makes me look mad. I recount everything.

"Wait a minute," he says, "haven't you been taking Clopezone for sleep? You were worried at your last appointment that you were beginning to get insomnia."

Yes, I had been taking it, and for longer than I should. He hands me a detailed patient information leaflet.

"Look at the side effects section."

Near the bottom of the list, under rare side effects, it says:

"Somnambulism with related retrograde amnesia. May include sleep driving and sleep cooking."

This takes a while to sink in. I crumple in sheer relief. Every weird thing in the past months was done by me, then wiped from memory on waking. I regret the £600 spent, and decide to hide my mouse at night in future. My first entry on Facebook was fucking weird, but the details corresponded with reality. I have a friend called Robin who shares the same birthday. I know a couple who built their own house and called it the tree house.

At least I don't own a car and am not interested enough in cooking to manage to burn the house down while inventing new recipes asleep.

I will never know what happened to Terence's court case, and no longer care. Though I found him hard to like, I don't think him capable of the malice I had imagined. My too long, too large relationship with Clopezone I ended, through a slow strangulation. No more malice in wonderland. Back from the mental river Styx.

I'll not take Clopezone again. Two therapist friends of mine piss themselves when I tell them I had bought a psychotherapy resource about dissociation whilst dissociated. I tried to get a refund but the organisation thought I was bullshitting.

Strange Odyssey

Before you decide you are mad, check what's in your medicine cabinet.

Rodina (Homeland), 1950s, automatic movement, chrome plated, USSR. This was the first watch made in Soviet Russia which has an automatic movement. Like the Poljot, it has a radial dial, but with the conventional arrangement for Arabic numerals.

Homeland

This story is woven of stories. It is not fiction. Fragments, shards, scars. Burning, screaming, crashing. From the wombland untimely ripped. Hope also. Finding connection. New home, new family. I have a part in this. Listening and encouraging. I want you all to know what is happening beyond these isles which partially decriminalised male homosexuality a half century ago, and in which my peers seek refuge. Not reportage. Personal realities.

I cannot tell you their names or where they come from. They are vulnerable and at risk of repatriation. I want you to feel what it is like to be them. Impossible.

One day I am sitting at my desk, reflecting. I have just assessed a woman who has been referred to Mind by her GP. In my preamble she picks up what I say about confidentiality.

"That's really important to me. You see, I feel I can't talk to anybody about this, because everyone knows about what happened."

I look puzzled.

"About five years ago one of my sons was involved in a crime which was so horrific it has destroyed my life."

She breaks down. I wait for her to recover.

"He was killed?"

"No, he was the murderer."

I've not come across a case like this before. I assure her we will do all we can to help her speak what has remained silent, and do the self-care she has felt too guilty to do.

As I am thinking I'm holding a card which was on the desk. It's for Mind Out, our LGBT service. The card's writer has just received her five years' leave to remain from the Home Office. Most of the card, with its simple printed message of "Thank You" is expressing thanks for us being her new LGBT family. Her family. The more I work with asylum seekers the more I sense that at the core of their experience is the loss of belonging, belonging with other people. Loss of place, less so.

Every time one of our LGBT asylum seekers gets leave to remain we rejoice. It's hugely significant. It means at least the possibility of rebuilding a life free of persecution.

Family, home, homeland. What are these to an asylum seeker?

I am running a therapy group for our LGBT asylum seekers.

Homeland

By now we have about eight people attending regularly. They come from across the world. Africa, Asia, Russia and the former Soviet Republics.

I have a reverie about a future world order which I will determine but in an entirely benevolent way. What happens outside the therapy room is I become fucking furious about what's been done to these people. It's a cliché, but how can it ever be wrong to love someone? Take note, I mean love, not desire sexually. I play rather late in life with the idea of becoming an anarchist. Bakunin and Chomsky sit unread on my bookcase. That really means on the floor where I ripped off the Amazon cardboard with zeal. In my ideal world there'll be an end to territoriality. The nation state will fade away. We will all be world citizens, saving a lot of money on passports and border forces. Religion can go too, and religion lite as in Buddhism. I'm New Ageist. But is homeland, heimat, call it what you will, where the heart is?

Marriage and religion. These torment me. I cannot decide. For many clients religion remains central to life. Some have a lingering doubt that their sexuality is natural. How could a loving God cause them such suffering?

My dream goes fluffy. There are itty bitty shitty things I'd ban. Summer garbage. Comic Sans font. Nougat, or nugget as we called it in Bristol. Nylon sheets, herring gulls. Okra, slimy rocks and pickled whelks. Toy dogs. Farting dogs. Cats with no fur. Cats with thin tails. Melanie Phillips and Gary Bushell. Ken Livingstone. Saying "back in the day". Abbreviations. Beginning any statement or answer to a question with "So". Airlines. Julie Burchill on days she annoys me, but not on days when she doesn't. Then I love her.

Yes, it's Julie Burchill who embodies all the contradictions I'm trying to live with, religion aside. If Israel doesn't offer her citizenship she can come and live with me in Stamford Hill, though she'll have to wear a wig and thick tights. For people of our age that might be fitting. Perhaps I'll try it on Purim, which is a carnival day. The problem is it's for the children and at six foot three I might seem whatever the Hasidic equivalent of a drag queen is. The golem in lipstick?

Trivia.

I focus on the group. It's last week. Yevgeny is watching his feet. Slowly he raises his head.

"I ... I moved from my home town ten years ago. No future there. However would I know another gay man? Things I heard about the West. Crazy and perverted they said. How could they let such people live?

"I went to Minsk to study for a degree in engineering. Still the screaming in my heart to find someone like me. I fell in love with a friend, but I was too afraid to say anything. He never had girlfriend. But how do I know?

"Then I found something online. A site where gay men could make contact, arrange to meet. It was dangerous if anyone saw these messages, but what else to do? I had finished my study by now, and working in the city. I had found someone online. He looked handsome, a nice guy. He was keen to meet me. I was little bit scared,

Homeland 101

but I decided to go ahead. What should we do? I suggested a café we could meet at in town. He said no, this was too dangerous. So, we agreed to meet in a park further out, where we would not be seen."

Everyone is listening intently to Yevgeny.

"As I got to the park it was just getting dark. A November day. I found him on a seat by himself. I was frightened but excited. The first time I ever meet someone like me. I sat beside him. 'NOW!' he shouted and everything is crazy. Three more men appear from behind a tree, and before I can do anything they have my arms pinned back. The man who is my date shouts 'You piece of shit' and thumps his boot into my groin. Then all is arms waving, fists crushing into my face, breaking my nose, grinding my guts and testicles. I'm losing consciousness. I smell and taste my own blood. The last thing I hear is, 'We haven't finished with you yet, queer, we know where you live.'

"I say this was first man I thought was gay I meet. How can I forget? No, first was Pyotr. We didn't feel sexual for each other. We became friends. We walked, and laughed, and talked about the world we wanted. He was always kind to me."

Yevgeny stops, his eyes welling up.

"Pyotr said he would stay with me at my apartment, to make me feel safer. He was kind man, always kind. For two weeks we were happy. One night heavy banging on door. 'Open up! Police!' I was shaking. The police hate us. I opened the door. It wasn't police. It was the

102   Watchwords

thugs who beat me in park. They pushed me back into the apartment, shouting 'Filth!' They began to beat Pyotr and me with clubs. We were screaming out for help, they were shouting 'Queer bastards!' For a moment they stopped hitting me and I ran. Just ran, ran. Out into the city.

"I woke up in alleyway. Somehow I found my way to my cousin's place."

The group say nothing. Yevgeny is still pouring from his jug of misery.

"One week later a call comes on my phone. Do I know a Pyotr Lobachevsky? I go to the address they give. It is hospital. Thank God, he is still alive. I expect to go up to the wards. Instead they show me to the basement. Too late I realise it is mortuary I am going to. Pyotr lies there. No part of his body is unbruised. The doctor says the cause of death is heart attack."

Stunned. All of us are stunned. Yevgeny weeps silently.

The asylum process. Simple on paper, logical, rational, beginning and end. Arrive in the UK. Contact the Home Office claiming asylum. Brief phone interview. Screening interview. Substantive interview. Given or refused refugee status.

At substantive interview you present a statement setting out your grounds for claiming asylum. You need to "prove beyond reasonable

Homeland 103

doubt" that you are lesbian, gay, bisexual or transgender, and that to return to your country would put your life at risk.

Seventy-five per cent of you will be refused asylum at this stage.

If refused, proceed to appeal to a first-tier immigration court. At this stage your chances of success improve to fifty per cent. If you fail, things get much more difficult. You can only appeal again on the grounds of legal errors made by the judge at the first appeal. Or you can try to launch a fresh claim, but this requires significant further evidence supporting your case since the first appeal. Things which have happened here, or changes in homeland legislation.

The group will discuss the process to help each other. It isn't what it seems. One person has been waiting twelve years for a first appeal. Someone else is getting their appeal heard within eight months of entering the country. Another two have leave to remain after their substantive interviews. But one of them was asked three questions about his statement. The other was grilled for seven hours, asked the same questions in different ways to see if he would slip up. I remember how it felt at immigration in Israel, and I was only questioned for about ten minutes.

You might think that hearing how someone else had what sounds like an easy ride with the authorities could produce dissent in the group. It doesn't, because of what it cost them all to get here.

This week. Patience is first to speak.

"We had been discovered in our dorm room by one of the security staff. We knew we had to escape. Voices in the distance, 'disgusting lesbians'.

"We got to the other side of Kampala and hid at Sheila's aunt's place. It seemed the safest way to get out was go by road to Nairobi, then fly to London. We went the next day and bought our tickets for the long-distance bus. We couldn't get seats together, so Sheila went and sat at the back.

"We got to the Kenyan border, excited and frightened. Our documents were in order so there were no problems. Sheila hugged me as we got back on the bus."

Patience falls silent for about thirty seconds. Wet-eyed, she begins again.

"It got dark. I fell asleep, a happy sleep. I was woken by sudden screaming, glass smashing, sounds of tearing. The bus was on its side. A truck with no lights had ploughed into us at a junction. I left Uganda with my Sheila. I left Kenya alone. Sheila died in the crash."

"My child", "my children". As LGBT people we come from families. Some of us have our own children. Most of the women I have met in the asylum seekers' group have left children behind.

Fatima begins.

Homeland   105

"My husband raped me. That's one reason I hate being in a mixed hostel, I only feel safe around women. I'm so worried about my daughters and what he might be doing to them. The older one is eighteen, so I have no grounds to bring her here. But the sixteen-year-old, I can argue to bring her here on grounds of family reunion. I have no money and I can't get any more legal aid so it is really difficult to find a solicitor. It could all fall apart because I run out of time."

What are children told? Clara doesn't know, because she has been refused all phone contact by her family. Whenever she talks about this there is a tangible sense of loss.

"I don't know if they will even remember me soon."

Elizabeth's story is less resigned, but raw.

"I'm still in contact with one of my sisters. She tells me what is happening, and it is all bad. When I ran away my son was three years old. Now he's six. He's living with his grandmother. My mother. She's a bad woman. She told him, when I didn't come back from travelling, that I had died of a disease. Imagine! As he became a bit older he learned that dead people were buried in the graveyard, and he wanted to know where I was. She went with my brother to the next village, and they found an unmarked grave, perhaps someone who died of AIDS. She took my son there and told him that is where I am buried."

I think back to the thank you card. Homeland is an illusion. Only connect. What if this is denied you?

Homeland

Omega Dynamic, automatic movement, stainless steel, 1967, Switzerland. Ulysse Nardin men's dress watch, stainless steel, 1941, Switzerland, mechanical movement. The back of the case bears an inscription congratulating the work of an inventor at the Swiss company Landis & Gyr.

Palm Sunday

Dynamic. The Church of England. Not credibly related. You won't see them together in a crossword clue, even the most maddeningly cryptic one. Cleave. That will be there. "Name a word with opposite meanings." Cleave together and cleave apart. This story delves into a cleavage in the Anglican Church, but it's for you to decide which kind is on display: sports bra or no bra.

Dynamism. Freud talked of unresolved conflicts in the dynamic unconscious. Here's a clue, but he wasn't specifically referencing Anglicanism. The Anglican unconscious depends on sherry and gin. No, what you will learn from me is conscious and sodden with malice aforethought. This isn't *The Archers*. If either sect dared enter the pub of the other, they would merely have thrown the darts at each other. I'll not say what would have constituted a bull's-eye.

Sect might sound a bit strong, but I'm only half joking. You weren't there in one kerfuffling and deeply eccentric corner of England thirty years ago. You may weigh the evidence.

Annually, four decades ago, Gray College Oxford's Chapel Choir ventured to the further shores of Anglican eccentricity. What I remember of Little Wretching and Blythe makes me think of an insoluble jigsaw puzzle which can only be solved using a mallet. This little corner of Norfolk is daintily odd, if not downright loony. The Church cleaved together two congregations who would rather insult each other from afar. One was Anglo-Catholic (High Church), the other Low (evangelical). Blythe had incense, enough to kill an asthmatic; Little Wretching had some recorders and a tambourine.

In readiness for each Palm Sunday the college chaplain led his choristers to these twin parishes who owed their livings to Gray College. Those who had been before teased us about what to expect, but we didn't believe them, as St Edmund's, Little Wretching, and St Chad's, Blythe, sounded straight out of E F Benson. I say twin parishes. This was not genetic. It was because an unfortunate priest/vicar had to be incumbent of both.

We were all aware of this divide. Gray College had been founded in honour of the Catholic revival in Anglicanism in the nineteenth century. I arrived in the college from the church at home which was Middle Anglican and inoffensive to all. The downside to this was there was no upside.

I could sing a bit so I joined the chapel choir. I was exposed to full-blown Anglo-Catholicism. I soon found myself enjoying all the smells and choreography. Though agnostic since, I still find myself occasionally wanting to go down on one knee and cross myself, for unrecognised reasons.

I soon discovered those who had been brought up in this tradition positively hated the Low Church. At Gray, the clearest manifestation of this was the Christian Union. They had electric guitars. They approached the College Chaplain to have a Rock for Jesus concert in the chapel.

The chapel choir had conniptions. How could such desecration be allowed? In the end the concert went ahead. I think this reflected the strength of character and genuine wish to include everyone that our chaplain possessed, despite what his private views might be.

All choir members were either High or sympathetic. At least there would be no fights on the way to East Anglia. What we didn't know was that our kerfuffle in the college was mere rehearsal compared to what we'd find in Norfolk. Father Jewell, the chaplain, had said something about the need for us to be equally friendly to all the parishioners. He didn't say why, nor did he use the language of diplomacy since he knew we were immune to it. While we felt ourselves adult, the inner children were wholly apparent to him.

It was the end of Hilary term (that's Spring everywhere except Oxford). Between the chaplain and the rest of us we had managed to get together enough cars and a minibus to make it to north Norfolk, avoiding Cambridge as far as possible. We were like excited children.

By British standards it was quite a long drive. Our usually meek driver amazed us by pushing his modest Renault to do a ton and we weren't even going downhill. The further we went, the flatter it became.

Our destination was a farm, ten miles from the north Norfolk coast, standing in magnificent isolation and slight dilapidation. It dated from the sixteenth century, and was painted cream with stuccoed "pinking", thatched on top. There were stables to one side, an old wooden barn, and even a duck pond, now mud, occupied by a pig.

"It's lovely. Straight out of 'Mummy and Neddy go to the Farm.' Does it have a name?" I asked.

Palm Sunday   111

"Wait until we turn into the drive." This was one of the return visitors. We were fortunate that Father Jewell ,a driver whose faith alone kept him out of the accident statistics, was ahead by some distance. James, driving our minibus, was the first to see it and swerved mid-guffaw, nearly destroying the sign.

"Gobblecock Hall Farm."

"All the women and half the men will like it," said James.

"I hope you aren't …" began Emmy before realising she was about to disclose her virginity and prudery.

Ralph, another second-timer, said, "The first thing you will be told by our host, Petronella, is why the name of the farm is noble, not risible.

Gobblecock is a perfectly understandable East Anglian term for turkey, of which many of the best are raised in this county."

"You said host. Is she the farmer?" I said.

"Not technically, but don't make the mistake of thinking she isn't your host. She's the matriarch of Blythe. She's hosted the choir about ten times now, and anyone who dared stand against her could face a similar fate to Saint Sebastian. That's just St Chad's parishioners. She wouldn't consider someone from St Edmund's to have enough brain cells. That said, we all felt that there's something about Petronella she doesn't want us to know."

I add, "That's an unusual name."

"Yes," returns Ralph. "It's a female version of Peter. So she's a rock. Around here that might be a flint, and she's flinty if someone dares contradict her."

"And," adds James, rather awkwardly, "If you take away four letters you're left with petrol. Explosive."

Emmy makes one more unfortunate sally. "Yes, but that leaves Nela, which isn't a name."

Petronella is leaning over the stable door to the kitchen. As it's sunny she looks as if she's put on her Barbour and scarf just to greet us.

"Helloo. So wonderful to have you back, my Oxford darlings. Come in, come in out of the cold. Don't mind the pig, she only bites on Fridays." It was Friday, so we walked round the other side of the vehicle.

The kitchen is vast, warmed by a range. Lawrence, whose father is an antiques dealer, is looking everything over very carefully. I can't tell from his face what he thinks, though his range of expressions suggest he would never win at poker, and if there are treasures, there's junk too.

Palm Sunday   113

"Before we proceed further, I have something to say. Gobblecock. It takes a lot of people by surprise, but with your intellects I'm sure it didn't. It's a noble name, not a silly one to snigger at. Snot flies out of James's nose mid-cough. The Gobblecock is simply the turkey rendered in our local dialect. I'll demonstrate." She grabs the saggy bit of her throat, pulls it back and forth and makes a sound like a zebra being drowned by a crocodile.

"The previous owner called it Hill Farm, which is silly almost anywhere in Norfolk. Come through to the parlour."

In the parlour we are introduced to Benton, the farmer. He is stout, about seventy, ruddy of complexion, and pissed. His sons burst in through the back door, Tim, Jim, and, more gracefully, Gideon. Ah, so they're who work the farm, I think to myself, maybe without needing Gideon, who might do something artistic. He seems an aesthete disappointed by life.

Petronella goes to the corner of the room and shouts up a steep set of stairs.

"Mummy, our guests have arrived. No, not Mr Trump the undertaker. The choristers from Oxford, and their chaplain, Father Jewell. No, he came back from Ethiopia four years ago."

"Abyssinia," shouts Father Jewell encouragingly.

"Caroline of Brunswick rode into Jerusalem on an ass on Palm Sunday," comes the faint reply.

"We won't disturb mummy now, she's very frail," her daughter tells us. "She welcomes you all. Right, tea everyone? Or is it a little too early for sherry?" It's 3 p.m.

"Come on, Mavis, you're needed in the kitchen," says Petronella to a woman who's just come into the parlour and looks like Petronella's skivvy.

"Mavis is Latin for Thrush," says Gareth, our autistic poet.

A few minutes later the women are back, Petronella empty-handed, Mavis carrying a tray of teapots. She goes back into the kitchen to emerge with another tray, this time of teacups and tumblers.

Petronella takes charge again.

"OK, blue pot Indian, grey pot Earl Grey, white pot Tio Pepe, and black pot Amontillado. Ha, perhaps I should say Poe Amontillado. I'm afraid we don't stoop to cream sherry at Gobblecock."

Now we know she's well read.

Palm Sunday   115

The teapots are all the same size, holding about a quart. The tea is served in fine willow pattern china cups, the sherry in the tumblers. I wonder, is this eccentricity, a performance, or a codependent alcoholic family? I look around the room. Tim and Jim are getting a lot of attention, and loving it. Rough. Two Heathcliffs. Gideon glances wanly at me and I look away. Please, not Edgar Linton.

An hour later we are all loosened up enough that our cheeky immature undergraduate comments flow. James says to Petronella, "So if this is Gobblecock Hall Farm, where's the cock, I mean Hall?" Petronella is momentarily puzzled.

"Hall and farm are the same thing, you see. You wouldn't have come to such a magnificent place as this had it been the tenanted farm of a grand house." Petronella appeared to believe this herself.

"Are you from here too, Petronella?"

"By now, yes, and I am Blythe." She's not as pissed as her husband, but catching up, and unaware of her unintended pun.

"You see, it all started during the war. I was a land girl sent from London and we were deployed all around the country, learning to farm just like the rural girls. I came here to Norfolk, Ioved Gobblecock, and very soon my Benton too. I was wooed to the sound of the nightingale, or another bird, and here we are, forty years later. You see, there were no nightingales in Sydenham."

"Sydenham?" asks Maurice, a second year who already knew about Petronella and Sydenham.

"Yes, it's in south London, near Lewisham. Have you heard of it?"

"No, but I imagine Gobblecock held greater allure." Some coughing.

"How kind of you," replies Petronella, oblivious. "Of course it did. We like to call it Warm Comfort Farm. We even have a parishioner who owns a Spitfire, which reminds me of being a land girl. You may get to see it. Gideon is booked for a birthday flight.

"I haven't seen my dear old childhood home in Sydenham since father was killed when a doodle bug landed on him. It didn't even explode. He was profoundly deaf. If he'd had a way of knowing the V1 had stopped making a noise he might have survived. If only he did not hear it coming. Mummy was in Knightsbridge, fortunately, or so she's always said, and she came down to live here after Benton and I married in 1946. It's a queer thought that she's ninety-three and still with us."

Cressida leant in to me and whispered, "I don't think we'll be seeing mummy, she might be a bit common." We never did see her over that weekend.

We were at the farm to be picked up by the various local people who had offered to help out. Residents of Little Wretching hadn't been asked. This wasn't because Petronella had forgotten. A number of

Palm Sunday   117

Little Wretchingers had offered to host, ignoring Petronella as usual. This was just as well as there weren't enough spare beds in Blythe, and Petronella had made the rare mistake of deputising the organisation of hosting to Daphne Trevis, who was wholly a pragmatist. Daphne knew exactly what to do; for example, to billet no one with Fred Loomis after the unfortunate incident a few years ago involving one of our sopranos.

Our hosts began arriving to take us home when a strangulated cry of "Petunia" echoed down the stairs and Petronella brushed past, saying, "I think mummy wants her flowers changing."

People had turned up with names on banners. Consternation ensued. Some had written their own names by mistake. Into the general melée stepped Father Brande, the incumbent priest in Blythe and vicar in Little Wretching. Apart from some unusual facial twitches he seemed sane. August, our student doctor, whispered something which rippled out. Such involuntary movements might be tardive dyskinesia, a side effect of antipsychotic medication. First impressions might have been misleading. Or maybe he had something stuck between his teeth

"Winston," he began, before remembering Father Jewell's name. "Godfrey, so wonderful to see you again with your melodious young people."

Vicars and rectors. Gobblecock Hall Farm, as embodied in Petronella, claimed to be the spiritual centre within the communities of the twin parishes. The boundary between was the Blythe Brook, or Wretching Brook, depending on where you lived. It was so tiny it had no official name. Little Wretching had a pub, with skittles and pool. Blythe had an inn, the Sorrell Horse. The Angry Sow in Wretching was in fact two hundred years older than the Sorrell Horse, but Blythers were keen to point out that the lumpy coat of rendering wasn't. The Angry Sow also had petunias in wire baskets. Worst of all was that the magnificent Queen Anne rectory was on Little Wretching land, where Father Brande lived in considerable comfort, with a much younger lodger, Roderick. The redbrick Victorian vicarage in Blythe, spacious but undistinguished, had been sold to a retired diplomat. It had a wonderful garden, like a series of gentle waterfalls. This was in distinct contrast to the bungalows surrounded by acres of flat lawn which seemed common in the area.

Tertius Brande was in his thirties, still felt he had a mission for God, and this would be only his second posting as incumbent. It certainly couldn't be odder than Suffolk. His predecessor had left under murky circumstances, and the diocesan bishop wanted someone with fresh ideas.

"We need someone gentle with a group of parishioners who can be a bit emotional." This was code for "involved in an internecine war", but the bishop didn't want to discourage Tertius.

The sad circumstances of his predecessor's leaving weren't so sad for the predecessor. He'd formed a marriage of convenience with Lavinia, a large, dominant woman with little desire for sex. She bullied. She had to be the judge of the annual flower contest. This always had to be held in the rectory garden. Life with Lavinia left the vicar listless. A vote at the parochial church council to move the flower show to the retired rear admiral's garden provided him with his opportunity. The next day he spent a gloriously viceful afternoon in a lavatory in King's Lynn before being arrested for cottaging. He went on to a more productive future in theatre design, and Lavinia was never heard of again.

Palm Sunday

"Right, before you rush off," began Godfrey, "let's just go over the schedule for the weekend and address any questions. It's all in your information packs. Thank you for your secretarial input, Emmy."

"That's her future summarised." This was Teddy, an outrider in the group as he couldn't intuit the boundary between humour and pure nastiness. We were rude, but never wittingly cruel.

"This evening you can relax with your very generous hosts."

"Hear, hear" with slurps of remaining sherry.

"Tomorrow we will be rehearsing in St Edmund's for the Saturday evening service, then you have the afternoon free. In the evening we are performing a sung mass. As you know, Holy Week doesn't start until Sunday, so this will be a usual mass. I think we're invited to the pub for supper afterwards."

"Which one?"

"The Angry Sow."

This was the social venue for St Edmund's, the obvious choice, but there was still an intake of breath from Blythe residents.

"On Sunday of course we rehearse in St Chad's for the main event", this to mollify those from Blythe.

"After that we've been kindly invited to lunch by Henry Lustral at the old rectory. Sadly we then depart."

You'd think this unremarkable housekeeping. It turned out that Little Wretching had been just as generous in hosting us as had Blythe, somewhat to the annoyance of the latter.

"Sung mass is something a long way above the heads of the Little Wretchingers who can just about manage communion and 'songs'". This from a rather world-soured older man.

Grumbling began. At one point a voice was raised, Grace Liddell from Little Wretching

"I think you've forgotten that Pevsner says the acoustics of St Edmund's are infinitely superior to those of St Chad's."

Margaret Beaver, whose property bordered Grace's at the stream, a gift from God since it prevented physical assault, came straight back with, "Oh, but Pevsner was stone deaf." She glanced round quickly in fear of contradiction at this guess. We were all sufficiently tired by now not to bother with it. I could imagine them pulling each other's hair.

Palm Sunday

"Grace, Margaret, I think this is not the time." Petronella had taken charge again, and swivelled her eyes at the door. We headed for release into the cool but pig shit-scented late afternoon air.

I'm to be staying with Clare and Maurice at the Ligusters. Maurice was there last year. He loves being leader and raconteur, is relentlessly funny, but a bit overstated, his unkempt beard and Balkan Sobranie saliva-dribbling clay pipes repellent. Over the years since then I've wondered if his brand of heritage pose continues among Oxford students. Clare went on to become a lesbian, living with her partner in rural Ireland. I'd always wondered if Maurice had played a role in the revision of her sexual preference.

Haus Liguster. It's on a slight rise and is indeed a house, not a bungalow. It's a bit like something begun by Le Corbusier and finished, say, by an abattoir designer.

"Who are my new guests, Maurice?" asks Hans Liguster.

"This is Clare, and Philip."

"Did you design the house yourself?" I consider a safe opener.

"Ah, no, architecture isn't among my accomplishments."

"Or the architect's," murmurs Maurice.

"But it's a bit of a clue as to my family heritage."

"Do you have a special way of keeping the lawn so ... precisely neat?" says Clare.

"Technology. Another clue to my family."

I dread what Maurice might say next, but he fails to stifle a fart and leaves things at that.

We admire the symmetry of the lawn, the vegetable garden, the tennis court. Everything is symmetrical. Even Hans's facial hair looks Prussian. The one exception is the oak tree, one of whose acorns was lucky enough to fall on the other side of the boundary fence and now grew in wobbly rebellious adolescence.

They've even managed to make themselves invisible to next door through a rank of perfectly aligned cypresses.

"It's a bit like Speer's cathedral of ice at Nuremburg," says Maurice. As I don't know what he's talking about I keep quiet, though I know it's rude to talk to Germanic hosts about the Third Reich. I'm hoping Hans has limited hearing. Hans heads for the house to help his wife with the Kaffee und Kuchen.

Palm Sunday   123

"When Hans comes back, ask him about Plexiplax baths," says Maurice.

"What?"

"Plexiplax baths."

The couple appear from the house with a perfectly performing tea trolley, gliding unlike any British product.

Frau Liguster introduces herself, "Hello, I'm Heidi."

"And these two are Clare and Philip," replies Maurice.

"Maurice was just telling me you have something to do with Plexiplax baths," Clare begins.

"Ah, you remember, Maurice. Yes, I am credited with the invention of the Plexiplax bath. Not Plexiplax itself, that has been around since the 1930s. Early attempts to make it strong enough to replace steel failed, but I finally succeeded in 1959. I always think it an irony that most of you British had one of my avocado bath suites long before you ever tasted an avocado."

"Plexiplax baths, how extraordinary," Clare manages to get out before any of us starts to choke, a usually unsuccessful attempt to disguise laughter. Fortunately the Ligusters seem too serious to notice.

"Invention runs in my family." No reaction from Maurice. This is new for him too.

"You see, my father is credited with patenting a number of inventions between the 1930s and 1950s. Mostly gas meters and electricity meters, for Landis & Gyr. I have a presentation watch given to him. Would you like to see it?"

"Yes please," I say, not to seem rude, to glares from the others.

He goes and collects a small round watch, with a chocolate brown dial and golden numerals and hands. On the dial it says Ulysse Nardin, Locle Suisse.

Hans turns the watch over:

"Here's the dedication."

M. H.

Für sehr gut bestandene

Lehrslingsprüfung

Palm Sunday   125

Landis & Gyr A.-G

1941

None of us is a German scholar. But I cannot help but feel uneasy.

As we are all quiet, Hans expounds.

"Ah ha, I know what you're thinking. Germany, 1941, gas meters, Nazis, Himmler." This goes far beyond what I'd been thinking and fills me with horror.

"Well, I can reassure you the answer of course is it is nothing to do with the Third Reich. You see, we are German-Swiss, not German. To be exact, the dialect we speak is Schwizertitsch. Landis and Gyr was in the German-speaking part of Switzerland. In 1942 it relocated from Switzerland to Australia. The dedication just means 'For Very Good Examination Performance'. I just like watching people's faces before I give the explanation."

Maurice decides not to leave it at this.

"You did sell an awful lot of watches to the Nazis during the war."

"Yes, that's true, my dear Maurice. But we sold them to you as well. We were neutral."

I hadn't thought of this as a benefit of neutrality before.

The couple take the watch and tea trolley back inside, then Maurice holds forth:

"Today, viewers, we will be experiencing architecture rare in its original setting, unique in Britain. Schwizertitsch Kitsch was accidentally created when two sets of architectural plans were muddled, one from the French, the other from the German part of Switzerland. When placed behind an Alp, the result is inoffensive. When transported to Norfolk as here in Haus Liguster, it becomes, like the typical Swiss product named for a bitonal bird, a great fat turd of a parasite on a nest."

With just enough time for us to recover composure, the Ligusters breeze out again to say we need to get moving back to Gobble to eat. We're looking forward to tomorrow, which is largely out and about and will mean not staying long in Mitteleuropa.

The rest of the evening is a blur. The Norfolk beer and cider is strong and delicious, straight from the barrel. I was expecting a samovar. Petronella had rounded up several strapping middle-aged women to sort out the rations, which consisted of huge plates of fish and chips. As Petronella said, "Not original, but local. The best."

Someone called Juniper, an old hippy, had been given the task of making arrangements for the vegetarians. She had spent rather too long, as Petronella told her, reading a book on Norfolk coastal

Palm Sunday 127

specialities. As there had only been one thing on Juniper's short list – samphire – and no one was prepared to help her gather nature's bounty, the veggies got coleslaw and gherkins instead. Benton managed to belch and say they were from Tesco before Petronella could stop him.

The only other event I remember from that evening was a wailing from upstairs. Petronella clearly preferred shouting to seeing her mother in person.

"Yes, mummy, we'll go shopping while the others are enjoying themselves in our fine county."

Another gurgling from upstairs.

"Mummy, how many times have I told you, they haven't opened a branch of Liberty in Fakenham yet. What? It's not in Knightsbridge anyway, it's off Regent Street."

Back at Haus Liguster we were all ready to flop. None of us fancied losing our Plexiplax bath virginities that night, so said we would try the avocado experience in the morning.

The Saturday morning rehearsal went well. The acoustic of St Edmund's was indeed good. Our only problem was my usual one. Emmy stood directly in front of me. Like Ella Fitzgerald, in one sense only, she inconsistently sang behind the beat. Attempts by Harry, our organ scholar, to correct this, had all failed, so he'd given up.

As we sorted out our afternoon destinations, Petronella made packed lunches for us all. Well, her assistants did.

To make the best of things (it was at least sunny and warm – a late Easter) we split between a group to visit Holkham Hall, and the other to Walsingham. I'd been to Holkham so went to Walsingham with the more pretentiously religious members of the choir. It's a strange place indeed. As you arrive it's like sliding into and drowning in a vat of incense. It boasts both Roman Catholic and Anglo-Catholic shrines, though the latter was a late arrival in 1938. It's one of the many places in the world in which people have been specially chosen for a visit by the Blessed Virgin Mary, in this case to be given an architectural lesson. Lady Richeldis was whisked off to Nazareth to be shown the holy house and asked to build a copy in Norfolk. It isn't Haus Liguster. The BVM left us unmolested, and the village offered attractive walks unmarred by denominational sectarianism.

The Church of St Edmund was the only thing in Little Wretching which looked down on Blythe, by virtue of elevation. It was flint built, with a round tower. Inside, elegant plainness with a simple hammer beam roof and worn oak pews. As in much of East Anglia there was evidence of target practice by Oliver Cromwell and his New Model Army.

We sang Byrd and Gibbons in the evening, with gracious congratulations after. We noticed many in the congregation who were new to us. I asked a beaming man as he approached about this.

Palm Sunday

"Ah, some of us admit to coming just for the music, and you are a rare treat, particularly when compared with Vox Clamantis in Deserto."

"Who?"

"Oh, you'll hear about them. Their musical director really did choose to call them 'The Voice of One Crying in the Wilderness'. I've a feeling Petronella may have given you a partial account of the two parishes."

As we milled around outside the church, one of the Little Wretchingers said "Coming to the pub, then?"

We poured into the Angry Sow to cheers, low ceilings, and billows of smoke. It's lovely to be so welcome when one expects the opposite. They couldn't give a fig for the Lady of Turkey Towers, as Petronella was known. In ruder mode her significance was described as a fart in a colander. All efforts not to get inebriated (we had, of course, the main event to do the next morning) went by the wayside and we were soon exchanging stories. Mostly, Little Wretching seemed more normal, if more alcoholic, than its rival. What I realised was that it wasn't high Anglicanism they disdained, it was the associated snobbery. We'd all been worried about Gray College's association with the Oxford Movement, but they hadn't even heard of it.

By Sunday morning Maurice, Clare and I had all been forced to have a bath. Truth was, we all needed one, but not with a travelogue. The Ligusters were scrupulous in their propriety, so there were no historical notes shouted through the door.

St Chad's in its valley was in striking contrast to St Edmund's. It was small. It was Victorian. Its style was unmistakably Victorian High Gothic, the sort of thing Ninian Comper might have designed if he'd accepted very small commissions. It was intended to be polychrome but they'd run out of one colour of brick so it looked strangely like a Tate exhibition. It was delightfully located. The spring flowers were in bloom. We readied ourselves to process with palms in hand behind Father Brande. There was a brief hiatus. To our immense relief the donkey had run away when Petronella went to collect him. She wanted to re-enact Jesus' entry into Jerusalem, starring her youngest son. The donkey had bitten her and she had a plaster on her left hand. Grace Liddell had her hair pulled when she said to Margaret Beaver that Petronella wanted her son to do a drag act as the sexually disinhibited Caroline. Blythe was very strident in support of Petronella whenever Gideon's sexuality was called into question. In private they knew the truth.

There was also a kerfuffle among the children dragged into Petronella's project who, ignoring the Church year, had been promised Easter eggs as a bribe to get them to play assorted residents of Jerusalem. The problem was that Gordon had found the box of eggs and hidden them around the church and grounds so they could have a treasure hunt. Gordon was the sort of precocious child whom other children, and some parents, wanted to slap.

Harry had chosen a Stanford setting of the mass which would go down easily in Blythe. Then, a favourite anthem of mine, "Drop, Drop Slow Tears", William Walton's setting, to keep us and the congregation challenged. We were happy that Father Brande was the celebrant, since it was sung mass and Godfrey sang a semitone flat, near the start of a service, sliding thereafter like dying bagpipes. I suppose it was an audible reminder of Jesus heading towards his end. When

Palm Sunday 131

Harry on occasion could stand it no more, and struck a note on the organ, Godfrey was totally oblivious, and the discrepancy all the more painfully apparent.

We emerged into sunlight and for a while differences going back to the Civil War between the congregations seemed buried. The expected coffee, tea and biscuits were matched by copious sherry in the church hall, though served conventionally from bottles. I had a suspicion again about the authenticity of Petronella's eccentricity.

The formal end to our visit was lunch *al fresco* in the garden of the one-time rectory, now inhabited by the Honorary Consul, or Henry, as he preferred. By the Sunday afternoon we had all been told, "He's our local colourful character." Someone must have created a list.

The rectory lawn was a relief, after the Ligusters', as a few moles had made their homes here. It was also clear that Henry believed in a balance between nature and order.

The occasion had been carefully choreographed by his wife, Isabelle, so there were polite little cliques sipping champagne when we arrived to gentle applause. We took our turns to be introduced, glass in hand, to Henry.

Henry had for twenty years been an Honorary Consul in northern Brazil. He loved the country, which loved him back. Two prizes had come to Norfolk with him. First, of course, his delightful wife Isabelle. Second, perched on his shoulder, a magnificent hyacinth macaw called Raul. The bird's disposition wasn't entirely clear from its face, which it turned at various angles to get a better look at us, interspersed with seductive hums, whistles, and alarming squawks. Henry stood in his smart linen suit and Panama hat, accessorised by some of his strawberry daiquiri and a couple of Raul's shits.

"Don't worry, he's harmless. If he likes you, let him hop on your shoulder and he'll give you a little kiss. If he doesn't he'll bite and we'll need the first aid kit. Although we've tried to teach him English, it's mostly filthy Portuguese, which at least I hope won't upset you."

"Arse bandit," agreed Raul.

The afternoon was delicious. We had sung well, but politely turned down the opportunity that evening to join the local choral society in a scratch performance of Stainer's *Crucifixion*. This was mostly down to our need to leave. Maurice said it was a bit unfair forcing Jesus to go through his passion twice in one week. The MD, Craven Ayes, was now oblivious to all references to tobacco and cigarettes, excepting "rough shag", which made him wistful. He still held sway among the elder residents of Little Wretching, but no Blyther would cross the threshold of the Wesleyan chapel, the rehearsal and performance venue. His choir was known by Blythers as the Reedy Warblers for reasons connected with age, not ornithology. This was Vox Clamantis in Deserto.

"He also has a scratch orchestra known locally as the Disconcertgebouw," adds Margaret.

Palm Sunday 133

Then there was a buzzing in the distance, too loud to be an insect. A few seconds later, over us flew a two-seater Spitfire, Gideon's birthday treat. Benton blurted, "It's Biggles and Ginger."

"Don't you dare, Benton," Petronella cried out, "you know there's nothing like that going on."

Garth, our poetry scholar, burst into tears. So did I, and several of the villagers. The sound of the Merlin engine caught us all off guard.

Perhaps it was a memory of parental memories, of being a child in the war. Garth could also imitate a Sopwith Camel and a Sopwith Pup starting up, taxiing and taking off, and was often asked to do so on drunken occasions which wanted World War 1 reenactions.

The Spitfire seemed to excite something in Raul. He had walked onto my shoulder and was taking a rather more thorough look inside my left ear than I would have liked.

"Cona, cona, cona," he screeched, flew around for a bit, then headed for Heidi Liguster and dumped a magnificent poo on her fascinator. Among screeches of bird and woman we howled as discreetly as possible. Raul's parting shot at Frau Liguster was "Filha da puta."

The two priests were talking. Raul landed on Father Brande's shoulder, walked down his back, commenting "Rego do cu" on the way. Once on the ground he stood between Godfrey and Tertius, looked up at both, and said "Bichas."

"Mmm." Godfrey is unsure what to say. "He seems to know the Portuguese for 'clergy.'"

This entertaining sequence of events ended when Raul returned to his master's head and started to rub up and down on Henry's bald pate. "Vou meter em vôce ate vôce gritou meu nome." Before this impressively long vocal climax is followed by anything else, Henry manages to run over and get Raul into his aviary. The verbal barrage continues, and ends with "Fuck off and die", presumably so we English speakers don't feel short changed.

Henry is still on good form.

"The downside is if we ever have Portuguese-speaking guests we have to find a tolerant parrot foster carer for the duration."

"Who taught him?" I ask.

"We don't know. I'm sure you're aware parrots can live for a long time. Raul may have already been twenty when we got him, and we were told he was rescued from a favela, which might explain his vocabulary. It's a scandal that many wild animals are being poached from the Amazon and sold as pets. At least Raul was already captive."

"And what about his English?"

Palm Sunday 135

"That was me. I found some choice phrases I'd like to say in person to colleagues in the consulate, then hear them at random to soothe me at the end of the day. Did any of you understand the Portuguese?"

"Well," Clare said, "I could work out from other languages that cona isn't ice cream, or coffee. The only Portuguese student in the choir is on his year abroad. As it was the, um, icing on the cake, would you tell us what the last thing was he said when you rushed him to the aviary?"

Henry thinks briefly. "Oh, all right, as you're the best guests I've had. Raul had a mate back in Salvador, who died. He was bereft for some time apparently, but when we took him on he transferred his affections to me. It's not unheard of with parrots, but it's better they should have a feathered mate, so as not to create mortifying social situations. What you witnessed was Raul masturbating while shouting, 'I'll fuck you until you scream my name.' It's odd, isn't it, that he has absolutely no idea what the words coming out of his beak mean."

"I don't like his vocabulary," said Emmy.

"You can't blame him," replied Henry. "You can't take the favela out of the bird. He did also improve in comportment when we stopped his Caipirinhas."

Emmy said no more, though she wanted to find out what a Caipirinha was.

"Wouldn't he have picked up a lot from Isabelle?" adds Maurice.

"Yes." The conversation ends here and Henry stalks off to this flower beds. Emmy goes over to Tiger, stretched languidly on the wall sunning himself. This is a reality check in an otherwise bizarre world. Tiger is a fat tabby cat, not a tiger, or jaguar, as he would need to have been in Brazil. Emmy gives him a friendly chuck under the chin, and he responds with a yowl and inserting all his sharp bits into her. We don't even pretend to be sympathetic. Poor Emmy. Yet her beige life probably meant she'd have the longest marriage of us all.

Henry comes back from closely examining a rose.

"Life in Brazil must have been so exciting," Clare says. "How do you keep stimulated in the English flatlands?"

"We have our highlights, such as visits from seats of learning. Then, one thing I hate is orchids, which made me feel I was near a hornets' nest whenever I saw them in Brazil – several times a day. My revenge here is to breed anemones; botanical ones in the garden and zoological ones in my aquarium, which I designed for them.

"Other than that I've made a specialism of trivia. Trivia as in *bon mots* and trivia as in pub quizzes. They don't really like it when I'm quiz master as I suspect not all rumours of inbreeding in East Anglia are groundless."

"Oh, try something on us, please."

Palm Sunday

"All right Maurice. When spelling Canute the Norwegian way, why is caution needed?"

Some ruffled brows, no suggestions.

"Because you might end up with Cunt."

"And a pub quiz question?"

"After briefly being employed to work on the screenplay of *Gone with the Wind*, what did F. Scott Fitzgerald answer when asked what it was like?"

"When he did what?"

"That's not an answer."

Perhaps because Oxford students thought they were worthy of higher intellectual pursuits, again there came no answer.

"He said 'it's like a whore's dream, just as long and just as pointless'. Personally I would say the same of *The Name of the Rose*. Or any book longer than a thousand pages."

"The Bible's quite long," adds Emmy.

"I think you've made my point for me, Emmy. One more for you. What links the literary figure Edward Lear with sexology?"

"Come on, Maurice, we must get the literary bit," I said. "The science is a bit Cambridge, or even continental. And Lear is nonsense too. Wait, where's our muse gone?"

Garth was enjoying a dogfight round the lilac, joined by a real dog, Jonquil, a French poodle confused as to which side to take.

"Garth, could you come and help us with our conundrum?"

"Oh yes, be right there."

Henry repeated the question. No hesitation from Garth.

"The Dong with the luminous nose."

"Semi-congratulations, Garth. Your Oxford schnozzle has led you to an obvious symbolic association. Being a Cambridge man myself I was counting on the science too. The real answer is compulsive

Palm Sunday   139

masturbation. Lear was tormented by this habit and its interruption of his literary pursuits and thus he became an historic note for the sexologists."

"Piss flaps," concludes Raul, and falls asleep.

On the Sunday evening we gathered back at Gobblecock for our farewells. On the assumption that no one had been acting a part, this weekend remained the most bizarre of my life. Even now, you only have to say Palm Sunday to a fellow traveller for them to repatriate whatever is in their mouth.

Petronella fussed around us with coffee and bags of alcoholic gifts. Then she reappeared with another tray of mugs, only these were empty.

"These are my artistic and musical son's latest enterprise. There's one for each of you."

A very sturdy piece of stoneware, stamped "Gray College Oxford" still holds my toothbrushes and razors. We thanked Gideon for his "Japanese Tea Bowls" and ask him about his flight in the Spitfire. He said he'd only vomited twice.

One other mystery was left dangling as we left. A very effortful "Knightsbridge" was screeched from upstairs. None of us ever did find out what mummy did near Harrods.

On the way home we dozed, related our surreal experiences to one another, and felt that our England was forever some corner of an alien field, ripe for ribaldry. Most of us belonged to a more silly than pretentious dining and party games society called the Moriarty Society. The cars were soon bumping up and down ripe with our ideas for Norfolk Nonsense, which we needn't steal from Debrett's House Party Games. Godfrey was our Senior Member.

As to the Anglican cleavage, we concluded it was both sports bra and no bra. In the end the hostility between the two parishes was really a game to keep life interesting.

In loving memory of the Rt. Rev. Geoffrey Rowell, sometime chaplain of Keble College, Oxford, who made this story possible.

Palm Sunday

Rolex Oyster Imperial Chronometer, 9 Carat solid gold, 1938, Swiss, mechanical movement. Before this watch was restored to its original condition in 2016 it bore the inscription 'To Bernard from Mary, 1939'. This was polished out by the restorer as buyers generally don't want personal dedications that were intended for someone else. An online search of the case number revealed an auction catalogue from 2016 in which the unrestored watch was up for sale, and the inscription was mentioned. But for this, Bernard and Mary would have been erased from history.

To Bernard from Mary, 1939

3 September 1939

Dear Bernard,

I'm sitting in our favourite place, watching the surging blueness slip in and out of Durdle Door. There were thunderstorms last night. This morning was pleasantly sunny. Now it is still sunny, but more heavy rains await, though the rumble hasn't started. I wonder if Durdle Door will revert to the volcano it once was? Our war with Germany has begun.

In the space of a day my enjoyment of Dorset is gone. It's like waking up and feeling unreal. All the details are there as before, but they are illusory. Just as other people think you and I can't be real.

As you know, in the evenings I have been venturing into Soho to see where the pansies and queers, sapphists and other phantoms go. I thought we were like them, but we aren't. The women desire women, even though they may adopt, or even feel, masculine attributes. I know that we are not really a woman. Of course, I cannot mention this to any friend; I would soon have none to speak with. I feel, though, that the demi-monde could offer some clue as to who we are. Most of the denizens say I am an invert, a butch. At least they weren't mocking. One of them, Dennis, overheard the conversation and approached me. We took a table near a basement window. He said I have met someone

To Bernard from Mary, 1939   143

like you before. Something was unvoiced. I'll see him again in London.

Tomorrow I shall go and see Corfe Castle one last time, then Clive will drive me back to town.

I'll write again soon,

Mary.

10 December 1939

Dear Bernard,

A fantastic lot has happened since Dorset, and it's not just the war. Still there aren't even distant rumbles for us. Warsaw has fallen. The Soviets have started bombing Helsinki, and we have hobbled the Graf Spee off Argentina. At home people have had their dogs and cats put down in tens of thousands rather than risk the ministrations of invading Nazis. They've closed London Zoo for now and destroyed some poisonous creatures, in case of a mass escape during a bombing raid.

Personally the Luftwaffe worries me more. Everyone is in a state of dazed trepidation.

This phoney war can't be worse than the real thing, only it is an enormous gaping maw to fill with unnameable imaginings. The

144   Watchwords

blackout is the worst of it. Though, I've noticed, in concealment can lie fulfilment. It seems that we, by which I mean all the exiles of love, are more numerous than I thought. When I was walking home near Victoria the other night I saw a police officer showing a man the way, and it wasn't to Pimlico. They looked aghast when caught by the full moon, so I winked at them before treading carefully on.

I've met Dennis several times now, and we are firm friends. This is because, rather than in spite, of what we each hold back. He looks like a mannish woman, of whom there are plenty, but there is something else.

I owe to him a revelation, for an astonishing one from him. Our world exists! Perhaps only the beginnings, but it is there. Dennis brought me some books when we met at the Two Swallows. Some were by a German called Magnus Hirschfeld. After the Great War he opened the Institute of Sexual Research in Berlin. He himself is an urning, an invert. His great project as a scientist was to advance our knowledge of sex and sexuality, and not see its variants as sick or depraved. He called himself a sexologist, as well as being a surgeon. This great man coined a term. Transsexualism. It means people born into a body at variance with the sex they know themselves to be, a sense often starting in childhood, and causing anguish which can't be allayed. This is us, Bernard!

Dennis made a further gesture I shall never forget. He handed me a book, an autobiography. Its title *Man into Woman*. My hands shook a little as I opened the cover. "An authentic record of a change of sex. The true story of the miraculous transformation of the Danish painter Einar Wegener."

To Bernard from Mary, 1939   145

I have since read it three times. Einar married. His attraction was to women, and this wasn't to change. He wasn't an effeminate queer man who wished to be like a woman. His destiny also was to become inwardly as well as outwardly a woman. He managed to become what we have been only in reverie. He left his native Denmark to consult with Dr Hirschfeld, the first person to take him seriously. Hirschfeld performed the first of several operations to turn Einar into Lili. Briefly the bud opened into flower. There is a wonderful photograph of Lili in the book, looking coyly from behind a fan, to all appearances a woman.

Other operations followed, but Lili's health weakened, and she died from infection in 1931, with Gerda, her wife, still at her side. Except for her untimely death, this is a story of such hope for us. How can the terror of history erase the good with such ease? Lili's book was published in English in 1933, the year Hitler took power and destroyed Dr Hirschfeld's institute, burning Lili's book with the rest. Thank God the good doctor had left the country before. You and I, we will become the old Berlin, where our sex and our desires can be a reality. The liberal Weimar Berlin which is so hard to conceive of now, the city of outsiders.

Christmas Day 1939

I wish so much to lay a lily on Lili Elbe's grave. Until this war is ended, and maybe not even then (who knows who will prevail), we cannot hope to reach Dresden where she lies. Again, Dennis came to my aid.

I mentioned the homage I wanted to make, the next time we met. At last he said it. He is woman into man! "I think that you are too," he said. "Yes," I said, "I am Mary and Bernard." Simple words, but a lifelong prison beginning to melt away. I told him I lacked his courage to begin to change myself. He said, this is only a costume. Let's hope that one day we have our own Dr Hirschfeld.

We shared our disappointment about not being able to visit Dresden. Henry had another suggestion. We would meet and go to Kensal Green cemetery. Bring a lily, he said, with no further explanation.

That morning we met at the tube station and walked along the wall of the old cemetery. Dennis didn't take me immediately to his chosen destination, but showed me the catacombs, and some of the other famous late residents. I'd thought them all to be in Highgate, but here were Thackeray, Trollope and Wilkie Collins, as well as leaders in other fields, such as Isambard Kingdom Brunel. Henry said there was a scientific connection in the memorialised person he had brought me to visit.

There was a simple stone, stating "Dr James Barry, Inspector General of Army Hospitals. Died 15th July 1865 age 71 years." The doctor had a distinguished career, including being the first British doctor to deliver a child by caesarean section where both mother and child survived. Then the surprise from Henry. The doctor had been known by other names: Dr James Miranda Steuart Barry, and, early in life, Margaret Anne Bulkley. When Barry died, a charwoman laying out the body discovered that he was anatomically a woman. He had managed to qualify as a doctor when no woman was permitted to do so, and went on to become prominent, if not eminent.

Dennis's eyes as well as mine glistened as I laid my white lily very gently before the stone.

To Bernard from Mary, 1939

I have something which I hope will outlast what comes; perhaps outlast us. It is a watch on which I've spent my savings, engraved from me to you, Bernard, in this year 1939.

September 1940

Dear Mary,

I live in a state of constant tension. Somehow I have survived while others no less skilled than I have lost their lives plummeting to earth.

We are strained beyond endurance, and the fresh pilots pushed beyond their capabilities. Only last week Duncan Spence died. It wasn't even in combat. He was returning to his airfield too late and got caught in a storm. In the dark he must have been disoriented and scared. His last radio communication was that he was pulling up to five thousand feet. When the wreckage of the plane was found, it was upside down. He had been flying inverted without knowing it and "climbed" metal-coffined into the soil. I know it sounds bizarre, but it's happened on too many occasions.

Summer 1941

Mary landed lightly and taxied the Spitfire to a halt near the hangar. Being an Air Transport Auxiliary pilot was the nearest thing to active combat she could achieve, and at least, as in a childhood dream, she could be a swallow in the summer sky.

There isn't much to add about Bernard and Mary. Only Mary is remembered, and by a very few. Bernard and Mary died in Bethnal Green underground station on 3 March 1943, trying to get into the bomb shelter. Human panic and crush were the cause, not bombs from the Luftwaffe.

The site of their grave is unknown. There was no one to identify the body. The watch on Mary's wrist was stolen.

In 2016 the watch, the only relic of Mary and Bernard, was sold at auction. The buyer had it restored. In case a future owner wouldn't want it, Mary's engraving was erased. Seventy-seven years later nothing was left.

These letters, the only record of Mary and Bernard, also do not exist. Mary carried them with her always. Now they exist only in your memory.

To Bernard from Mary, 1939   149

Hamilton K-475, automatic movement, gold filled, USA, 1961. This is one of a series of watches created by Hamilton's most celebrated designer, Richard Arbib. His signature style is asymmetric cases with a union of art deco and space age elements. He designed the Hamilton Ventura, the world's first battery powered watch, released in 1957. Elvis Presley owned two of these, the second of which he bought for himself in 1964 and kept until his death.

A Fine Timepiece

It's 2005, somewhere in the county of Suffolk. Joanna and Ian, my brother and sister, are here for Mum in gorgeous May. The grandiose wisteria is a lilac-shaded cap for the roof, fully in its glory, like jacaranda pouring out the heady scent I remember from Malawi. It should be pruned say the prudent, but what was the Virgin Queen without her wig in her prime? Just where Mum sits beneath it, a gently cooing collared dove nurtures its brood. Both adults return each year to the tender feeding my mother gives them.

I am happy again, the enblackening curse of depression banished for a while. The drone of the bees is what I miss most in London, and butterflies. In the tides of crowds I feel as insignificant as a butterfly. The depressed attract inattention.

"While you're all here, there's something I'd like to do." I know Mum's been wanting to say something. "I've decided it would be a good idea to take out a power of attorney."

We look at one another. Of course it's sensible, but unexpected. I ask the question.

"Mum, I think it's a good idea too. Any special reason you want to do it now?"

"Not really, it's just in case I go gaga one day." Practical, to the point, her usual style. We settle down with the paperwork the next day. A neighbour kindly acts as witness.

Five summers on, a July visit. Hoverflies, hollyhocks against the rectory wall, and I'm still enjoying *Don Quixote* as I turn pink in the heat. How many more summers like this? That shuddering phantom in my spine. *Et in Arcadia Ego* – death in the summer bees' drone. Whose death? This village may forget us soon, leaving only a stone in the churchyard abbreviating two lives. Our own future erasure I push below full consciousness.

I'm going to my car to leave, when I remember. "Mum, how is Fiona these days?" Fiona is my mother's aunt. She's a lovely, effusive woman who fussed over us as children in the days she was matriarch of the family farm. And she made the best sherry trifle. A few years ago she'd winked at me and said, "I thought you'd like Brighton."

"She's fine, I think. Why do you ask?"

"You haven't mentioned her for a while, Mum, and I was worried her MS might be getting worse."

"MS? I didn't know she had MS!" It feels like an electric shock.

"Mum, it was you who told us. Maybe twelve years ago."

Silence.

Who to fucking talk to? Cunting hell. Marcus, yes, Marcus. His mother has Alzheimer's, he's been looking after her for years. His brother a waste of space but he gets all the love. Shit, what will it be like for us? She must have known something when we did the power of attorney. Did I notice anything strange then? Ask Ian, my brother, he only lives up the road. No. Marcus will tell me where to look for help. Try to get a diagnosis – GP, Memory Clinic, what after? My thought skewers on the road ahead. Sky lowering to charcoal, spots, now rain deluge. Wipers on. Can hardly see. Ominous music from the radio. What? Something terrible coming. Don't crash now. An announcement. Classic FM, Featured in Film. Question: which film would make you never want to shower again? Fuck you very much Bernard Herrmann on a day like no other. No one will mummify my mummy – what a terrible word. I hate myself.

I am calmer, back in London. Everyone urges restraint. We don't know what's wrong yet. One of my psychiatrist friends says it could be any of many things. Look for problems in recent recall, that's the most likely indicator of dementia. Your mother forgot something which happened twelve years ago. Anyone might do that at her age.

A reverie. Mum's sense of humour sometimes was absent, at others inventive. She gave me a pencil sharpener in a shoebox for Christmas one year. She thought this a lot funnier at the time than did I aged eight. Then when she cleverly hid Easter eggs in the garden for us to find the mice got there and ate them first so she had three wailing monsters to pacify. I wish, I wish she could have shown her hurt under the beetle carapace which shielded her. Throughout her life she bore a trauma she carefully hid. I'm surprised she was never, as far as we knew, depressed. Like many women of her generation she bore her

A Fine Timepiece

pains and endured.

Her father, Stanley, went to Shanghai in 1929 to work as a police officer, and relieve the money pressures on a family of six children in a poor Suffolk village. He met a pretty Eurasian woman and Mum was born in 1931. In 1934 he had his first home leave, and came back to England, leaving my grandmother in Shanghai. A great sea voyage when my mother felt too hot and threw her coat into the Suez Canal. We have a photograph; a little girl in a white dress on a tricycle, the deck of the ship, her smiling as he presses the shutter. What my two-year-old mother didn't know is that there was a plot between her grandmother and father that she be left behind in Suffolk to grow up British. She saw her parents twice more during her life. She could never forgive the abandonment; nor would she ever have considered seeing someone in my profession, psychotherapy. Her mother, Louise, suffered too, not knowing that Stanley would return without their daughter.

My psychiatrist friend shows me how to do a Mini Mental State Examination. Not diagnostic, but used to check for memory loss. It might be worth trying, at least until Mum gets a proper medical assessment.

I take some copies of the MMSE with me at Christmas.

What I don't understand is why the questions are of equal weight. Mum knows where we are, on which floor (it's a bungalow, so not difficult), the year, and that it's in the afternoon. When I show her my watch, she identifies it as "a fine timepiece". This, I've been told, is the wrong answer and scores zero. I fume at this injustice. I want to confront whoever concocted this fucking thing and torture him into

154   Watchwords

admitting he was wrong.

Mum can follow the instruction to fold a piece of paper in half and put it on the floor. I almost cry when asking her to do this.

She gets all the recent recall questions wrong – shit – yet just manages to pass the test. How? Things are not normal.

"Something's been taking the food for the doves," she says.

"Pigeons?"

"No, these don't have wings. Brown animals, quite big." My sister and I are stumped, until Penny, one of Mum's old work friends drops in. She asks for a quick word with us as Mum goes to make tea.

"I'm really worried about your mum. Did she tell you about the rats?"

"The what?" my sister says. "Are they what's been eating the bird food?"

"Yes, and I'm worried they might be getting in the house."

Joanna begins to weep. "How can she possibly not know? She's been

A Fine Timepiece   155

morbidly afraid of rats all her life."

"Cows too" I add, irrelevantly.

I come back in February. We don't know how much time we have together. I look out into the garden and realise it isn't just winter. The garden has died. Its guardian, like the Cheshire cat, is evaporating, but it isn't the smile which is left. This garden has been Mum's pride. Since retirement she has spent her loving care on it, and it has been a delight for all of us. Now she doesn't even look out of the windows, still less want to go outside. The garden feels to me like her inner world, chaotic and moribund.

I try writing to her GP, asking that he raise the subject of memory at her next appointment. He refuses on the grounds of patient confidentiality. It is my bolder sister who contacts the health centre by phone and insists on being heard.

We sit with Mum and the psychiatrist, fearing the diagnosis. She is told that she has vascular dementia. Mum, a retired nurse and midwife, hears this and just swings her legs like a little girl. I don't know who she is.

We're home again, shell-shocked, except for Mum. An occupational therapist will come round to make an assessment. The psychiatrist has prescribed Aricept, even though he and I know it's too late to have any effect. It would already have been too late before she forgot about Fiona's MS. It's always too late with dementia.

Mum comes back from the kitchen a fifth time after finding she's already made tea.

"Mum, can I do one of those questionnaires again with you?"

"One of those funny test things?" I'm surprised she remembers.

"Yes, if you'd like to?"

"Well, that nurse who looked like a lesbian traffic warden did some silly tests, was it today?"

"Yes, Mum, and she was an OT, not a nurse, or a traffic warden." I'm annoyed I wasn't around for the OT but I'll ask Joanna and Ian what happened.

As before, Mum got all the recent recall questions wrong. "Swing, er, rope, um … lesbian."

"No. Bat, ball, cap."

Joanna is back with more tea. I dread what will follow. I'm half tempted to pick up a pencil and spare my own feelings.

A Fine Timepiece

Slowly I reach down and take off my watch, so Mum can't see what I'm doing. I hold it up to her.

"What's this, Mum?"

"It's a watch. It's a very fine timepiece. Very fine."

Christmas 2012

Since 1992 I have never been home for Christmas. Dad died the following January, and Mum never felt like having Christmas thereafter. With a measure of guilt I chose to spend Christmas elsewhere. Mum's birthday was on 27 December, a recipe for disappointment in her childhood, but we always went to see her then.

In 2012 I had no plans. I knew we were nearing the point of having to activate the power of attorney and find supported accommodation for her. Ian had resigned from his job as she wasn't safe to be left alone in the house. She never went out, and the orbit of her life swept ever inwards. Ian had hidden the car keys, but by now she wouldn't even have thought of driving.

I remember arriving and feeling as if I were entering a mausoleum. Mum never liked showers, but had a daily bath as she would have firmly advised a patient to do. It was clear she had stopped bathing. The house had that sickly rank smell. I think Ian was so used to it he no longer noticed. She sat hardly speaking. This was worse than endlessly repeated questions.

A phone call from Penny. Very worried. Mum had pushed her away after a misunderstanding. She didn't like living in the village any more. We knew this. We didn't know, and she never said this to us, that she no longer wanted to live.

Joanna arrived on the 27th, and this was always when we exchanged presents. I had been a member of the Pink Singers in London for nearly twenty years. We had just recorded a new CD which I gave her for her birthday. My emotion crushed me. She absolutely loved it, and she played it over and again. I also felt shame. I had never invited her to one of our concerts, feeling she wasn't part of that part of me. At least I can say to the Pink Singers that we collectively gave my mother the last occasion I saw her genuinely happy.

2013

The black dog is back. I've had depression episodically for twenty years, and no longer can see what brings it on. I remember praying, or getting as near to it as an agnostic can.

"Please, Mum, don't die while I'm depressed."

On 18 March the phone call comes. My brother had never phoned me on a weekday afternoon, so I know immediately she's died. I remember crying for her for the next two days, through an alcoholic haze. I wish, I wish, I wish I'd been able to stand staying with you for more than three days as you became grouchier. I wish I had wanted to accept

A Fine Timepiece   159

your offer to take us to Shanghai twenty years earlier. I wish you'd let someone help you in your own pain.

There is one strange comfort. It wasn't the dementia that took her in the end. She had an aortic aneurysm. We knew of a family friend who had died in this way, in agony. In Mum's case, she seemed to have gone peacefully in her sleep. Ian told me she was lying on her back with her hands folded over her chest, like a pharaoh.

She died at a time when she was still living in her own house, and she knew who we were. The feared disintegration over many years wasn't to happen. In a sense, her timing was immaculate.

When the funeral director came to collect Mum she said, "Of course I remembered the name; your mother brought my first child into the world."

The funeral was set for 3 April. I was still very depressed, and took the awful decision on the day not to travel to Suffolk. Instead, I went to Southend and sat on the pier with a friend whose mother had also recently died. At 3 p.m., the allotted time, I spoke out loud to her over the sea.

"Mum, I will miss you for the rest of my life."

The funeral was for immediate family only. A memorial service in the village church was arranged for 20 April and, thank providence, I was well enough to attend. Somehow the trauma goaded me to action, through the need to support my brother and sister. There's no rhyme or reason to depression.

It was a beautiful sunny day. The three of us each offered our memories, and I had persuaded a midwife friend of Mum's to say something about her. That was a blank for us, and perhaps a selfish request by me. Mum was always scrupulous about patient confidentiality, so never brought her work home. She was liked and respected as an "old school" nurse. When asked by a nervous patient what to do, she was reported as saying, "stick your legs in the air and push."

During the service something was distracting me. On the church window to my right a tortoiseshell butterfly was beating its wings frantically trying to get out. When we'd finished, I waited until everyone else had left. Then I cupped the butterfly gently in my hands and carried it out of the church. I said "Look!" to everyone and opened my hands. The butterfly waited a couple of seconds before flitting away to freedom.

"Goodbye, Mum."

The little white dress

Mum was to see her parents only twice after 1934. She had a younger brother, Louis. He was born in Shanghai and went with his parents to Vancouver for Stanley's second long leave. This was October 1939, and they had to remain there for the duration. There's a photograph. A smiling young boy in a plaid coat and furry hat, sweeping the snow

A Fine Timepiece

from a suburban driveway. He died when he was ten. He had a brain tumour. Mum only ever saw his ashes, brought back to England after the war.

In 1956 Mum went to Montreal to work as a nurse. She didn't want her parents to know she was there. They were still in Vancouver. Someone in Suffolk had written to let her parents know, and Louise phoned her. Mum was furious, but she did cross the country to stay with them, and tour Oregon with Louise.

My brother, sister, and I drew closer as we worked to empty the family house of forty years, a travail. Ghosts emerged. Joanna found three things which burst our understandings of the past. She slept in Mum's bed, and found an envelope slipped between the mattresses. It contained photographs of her childhood, in China and in Suffolk. There were also pictures of her parents, with her and without. She was keeping these close to her, even in her last days.

The second item was a letter, sent to her in Canada by her aunt Madge. "Please don't be too hard on your mother," it said. "She was the subject of a cruel deception. Imagine one day that you may have a little girl, and what it might feel like to have her taken from you?" We checked dates. She received it in Montreal before travelling to see her parents for the last time.

"You remember the suitcase with Mum's wedding dress in it?" asked Joanna. I did. I think either Mum had shown it to me when I was a child, or I had a look while snooping.

"There's something else in it." I didn't remember anything else being there.

162 Watchwords

Joanna went to get the case. She opened it. There was the wedding dress. She took this out and unfolded it. Inside was a little girl's white dress. The dress she had worn on the ship from Shanghai, smiling at her daddy for the photograph. Mum had kept this, never mentioning its existence, for almost eighty years.

Sometimes it creeps up on me. Every time I remember the little white dress I weep. I can only think it connected Mum to the childhood she never had, and the parents she felt had abandoned her to exile.

Her stoicism was also her failing. Hearing about her emotions felt like the very beginning of snow. A few flakes fell. "I didn't have a very happy childhood" was one of them. Growing up in a Suffolk village in the 1930s and 1940s, the only child who looked different, she suffered racism. For the rest of her life she was unable to take pride in her Chinese heritage.

She could be absolutely infuriating, or very kind. Her suffering could be etched on her face. My friend Paula noticed this. "I can see the pain." I was so used to seeing pictures of Mum that I didn't notice it. Now I can.

She never thought she needed help; that to seek it would show weakness. I knew it wasn't going to happen. I saw the calcification throughout the twenty years after dad's death.

Among other memorabilia I have two special things which were hers. She attended the first run of *My Fair Lady* on Broadway. I envy her that. Throughout childhood I played the record with the funny cover: George Bernard Shaw as God, dangling Rex Harrison like a Pelham Puppet, in turn dangling Julie Andrews. For her eighty-first and final birthday I found the cover of the book in an art shop, as a reminder of her youth. After her death it remained unframed. Now it hangs on my bedroom wall, next to a sunset watercolour of a barge on the Deben at Woodbridge, one of her later works. We teased her about her early work. We had no idea how skilled she had become over the years. I never could, and never will, be able to paint.

Edele stainless steel and chrome plated men's watch, unbranded mechanical movement, 1970s, Swiss. Edele was one among many names created to label watches ordered in bulk from major manufacturers. There is no history for these watches as their maker is unknown. This one is NOS (new old stock), in other words, never previously sold, so in pristine condition.

Nineteen seventy-nine

Operation Yew Tree is a name chosen not to relate to its subject matter. The long bows of the English at Agincourt and old churchyards don't seem connected to historical child sex abuse. It's easiest to begin this with a distracted thought. An Independent Inquiry into Child Sexual Abuse lurches on with changes of chair. The great difference now compared with the history referred to is that it is spoken about, has revealed so much that it can turn you off to the true horror which has been uncovered.

I think, do I know anything from my own life which could be a matter of sexual abuse never before uncovered? I'm sure nothing happened to me. I often have clients who think they may have been sexually abused, have dissociated from the events, and this horror seems the only possible explanation of the inchoate distress in their lives. Some of them are right.

I remember something. The more I remember the more I fear its consequences, since they form a narrative very different from the publicly accepted one. I think I may have known someone when I was sixteen who as an adult I would feel very uncomfortable around. And another person for whom I have mixed feelings.

There was a fourteen-year-old boy, Ben Timbers, and a young teacher, Mr Graveney. And I was a closeted sixth former.

Ben Timbers

I'm fourteen, I'm Ben, and I'm different from other people. They say different, I say special. I might be gay, but that's not the main difference. Being weak is the worst thing. It makes me despise other people. I'm strong and I love my strength. This is the third school I've been to in four years. I blame my stupid dad for being in the RAF and moving all the time. I've learnt how to be from him. Mum is weak and disappears for a "little cry" now and then. I can tell that Dad's motto is "If you don't put yourself first no one else will." That's been a good way to look at things. At least I have no brothers or sisters to get in my way.

I don't understand what everyone looks so worried about. At the last school they took me off to see the psychologist. After he'd asked me some stupid questions like had I ever been cruel to a pet (we've never had pets) he brought Mum and Dad in. He said I had behavioural problems, and a condition called Conduct Disorder. Farty science for bad behaviour? So what? I was expelled from the school anyway.

I'm bigger now, a teenager, but no acne. That's really important. The thing is, I've realised I'm beautiful. Really handsome. I have unmarked olive skin (one good thing Mum gave me), green eyes, long eyelashes, and a full mouth. I'm seeing the effect this is having on others. Muscles are beginning to emerge, and my bum is curvy. I'm top of my class too. I'm Superman.

I can't know what girls think about this, because this is a man's world.

Nineteen seventy-nine

I'm looking in the bathroom mirror when Jennings dawdles as he passes, pretending to look at his own reflection.

"God, you're ugly," I say. "And stop looking at my arse, queer."

Every now and then I let Jennings play around with me. I see the hunger in his eyes. We have to find an unused classroom. It's never completely safe. The school is in town, so no fields or woods to conceal us.

I won't let him kiss me, and he always has to do what I ask. It ends in him giving me a blow job. I can see the spaniel-like adoration in his eyes. It disgusts me. After I spurt over his face if there's even a hint he's come himself I slap his face hard, once from each side. I can see the pleading "why?" in his face so I leave quickly so as not to kick him too. I don't want to leave marks.

My greatest satisfaction is that Will Shears is in the next bed to mine in the dorm. After lights out, he often stays awake as along as possible. I pretend to sleep. After a while I push down the bedclothes and gently stroke myself as if still asleep. Soon a rapid shuffling of bedclothes begins. A tossing culminating in a loud sigh. Poor Shears, such a lack of self-control. He is often loud enough to wake others and draw their laughter and scorn. At this point I "wake up" and look softly and fondly at him, never joining in the abuse. This gives me such a kick.

After a year in this school they know to respect me. No one calls me queer. Two boys have broken noses from when they have fallen against

168   Watchwords

the porcelain of the communal urinal. Then there was Gittings, two years senior to me, who made the mistake of calling me pretty boy, and catamite (he was doing Latin). At the time I had just joined the school archery club, which practised in the school yard. I slipped on the cobbles and Gittings got an arrow in the left buttock.

Brendan Graveney

Queen Anne's is my first teaching position after qualifying. I'm here for a probationary year. I studied in Bristol, so Bath was very convenient. I'd been to a selective day school, but not a boarding school. I'd always had a fantasy about the boarding world. I could have the experience of being a boarding master, while still having my university friends and a social life away from school. Let me be corny. I had great expectations. I was only five years older than some of the boys. I felt I could be master and chum at the same time. I could also pursue my personal fantasy.

My fantasy. I'm gay, and have always known this, have had a few boyfriends and gay friends. But I belong to a particular tradition, which goes back to Ancient Athens. I recently found a very useful book on this in the City Library, called *Greek Love*. In ancient Athens young male citizens were expected to take adolescent boys as lovers before they went on to get married. These relationships were exalted. Greek Love made a contemporary argument that such relationships could be an appropriate vehicle for adolescents to learn about sex, whatever their preference might turn out to be. The Greeks validated something we now call pederasty or paedophilia.

It's the Greek ideal I seek. There is something about boys between

Nineteen seventy-nine

puberty and adolescence, say 13–15 years old, which I find utterly beguiling. This is not paedophilia. I would never do something to a child who couldn't give consent. I only want the love of a youth whose love I can return. This is why I applied for the job. Really. I only have love to offer, so the danger will all be for me, if I am discovered, but it feels worth the risk.

Mr Graveney becomes friends with some of us in the sixth form. He introduces us to the radio broadcasts of *The Hitchhiker's Guide to the Galaxy* during our lessons, for illiterate science students. As boarders we get opportunities to go out and socialise at the weekend, with him *in loco parentis*. On one evening we have a cinema visit. I'm invited with Dave Simpson. I can already sense some kind of kindred spirit thing with Mr Graveney. It isn't sexual though. Neither Dave nor I seem to be on his sexual radar. I know about myself. Dave I'm not sure about, but he is ever with the handsome Darren. There is a kind of semaphore and an occasional wink to me from Brendan, but I feel utterly safe, like it's our secret, and thank providence there's one person I can go to who understands my difference.

We go to a pub in the city centre which is filled with men in jeans and leather jackets. I know that The Elephant is Bath's best-known poof pub. Mr Graveney's friend Jack is there, and greets us effusively. He is camp and in his fifties, so I wonder briefly how the pair know each other.

The film is screened at the arthouse Gandolfo, as it has not been passed by the censor. It is Pasolini's newest film, *Salo, or the one hundred and twenty days of Sodom*. Mr Graveney points out that the local paper has advertised it as *Salo, or the one hundred and thirty days of Sodom*, giving us ten extra days of Sodom free.

I didn't have the mental apparatus or stomach aged sixteen to appreciate the film's historic symbolism. From the story of four libertines torturing teenagers in Mussolini's last bolthole, all I can remember forty years later are two scenes. One is of adolescents being led like dogs on leads, force fed meat filled with nails, and the resultant screams and bleeding. The other scene is of a group sitting in a turd-filled cauldron. Repellent.

This raises a first question mark about Mr Graveney for me. Why would a teacher want to take two sixteen-year-olds to this?

The film over, we went back to Jack's flat, where I remember us being plied with gin and tonic, and Dave ending up on Mr Graveney's lap. Perhaps I was the only safe one after all. I didn't know if I liked this or not.

Jack said, "I've seen that Timbers boy you told me about, Brendan. What tarts they are at that age. Ripe for plucking and fucking." Jack had a laugh like a hyena. My skin crawled.

I don't remember any more of that evening. I was too drunk. The next day Dave was noticeably quiet. I wanted to know what he'd made of the experience, but didn't dare ask.

Durdur was wandering about with a mouth full of toothpaste.

Nineteen seventy-nine

"You look like you've been giving a fire extinguisher a blow job."
Durdur was another of Ben's choice victims. "I can't rinse, the tap doesn't work."

"Look what you've done, spots of your white toothpaste cum all over me, you filthy fairy. Come with me."

Ben dragged the weakly resisting Durdur into a cubicle, shoved his face in the pan and flushed. "You're drowning me," Durdur wailed.

"If I was you'd be dead by now, you feeble cunt." Ben had time to exit before a prefect arrived and also laughed at Durdur.

Ben

With some of the prefects I've seen that look in the eyes. Like they want to eat me. In the showers after rugby. I think there's some stuff happening in the cubicles but I can't be sure. Risks of getting caught are high.

One day we're back after games and I've gone to the music practice rooms. Burns comes in, fresh and ruddy from his shower.

"I thought I'd find you here."

"Well, here I am."

He wasted no time. He strode over and grasped me into an animal kiss. Then we both reached to undo our trousers. Cock rubbed on cock, mutual hand jobs. After a while I grabbed him and kind of wound all over him like a constrictor snake. He moaned, I moaned, this was great. In the end he told me to close my legs and thrust and came between my buttocks. He even stopped to finish me off too. If this is sex it is great. It also opens doors I hadn't imagined.

"We can do this again."

"Fuck yes," I said.

"But I'll kill you if you tell anyone. I'll kill you."

I'm a big game hunter. Burns and boys I can bully are one thing. I could land a far larger catch, one that can give me much more. A couple of times Mr Graveney has asked me up to his rooms with two or three of my classmates. All the prettiest boys. He gives us cans of beer and we watch the wrestling on TV. I catch his eye from time to time as I rub my cock. I arrange to end up face down on his bed, propped up on my arms to watch the pantomime antics on the TV. The wrestlers have names like Big Daddy and Giant Haystacks and are as sexy as the turdiest junior boy.

When I say the prettiest, most handsome, there can only be one, and it's me. We're quite noisy, so we might raise the suspicions of other boys and masters. I hush things up. The time's not right.

Nineteen seventy-nine

A month later I go up to his door on a Sunday afternoon. He's not the master on duty, so won't have to be doing the rounds. I do my five knocks.

"Come in, Ben."

The familiarity is unique. In class we are all known by our surnames, and it's only the sixth form who are allowed their first names at the weekend. I'm in. This Sunday I am alone, and have a couple of hours before I need to be anywhere else. We look at each other, and he walks softly across the room to me. Our eyes gaze into each other's. I let my full lips part slightly. Then I jump, my arms around his neck and legs round his waist.

"I want you so much."

"Me too."

We snog for ages. We tear off each other's clothes, then fall into the bed. I won't describe it. We broke the law in a number of ways, and kept going for an hour. He tired first. At that age I could repeat orgasm frequently.

We must both have napped for a few minutes. When I woke he was staring fondly in my eyes. What he didn't know was that his symphony was my overture. My overture and enchantment. As this isn't a pornographic story you can stop reading now if you think there is going to be more sex.

"You've done something wonderful for me. And I was right, you wanted it equally."

"Yes, that's true. But there's something else you can give me."

"What is that?"

"Five hundred pounds."

You'll wonder, did he pay? Five hundred pounds was a lot in 1979. He did pay, but in a different way. I can't know what happened in full as our lives were soon to part.

Mr Graveney came storming through our dorm.

"He's suspended me."

"What?"

"The head's suspended me. For inviting boys to my rooms. What did he think I was doing, fucking them?"

Nineteen seventy-nine 175

I was sympathetic as I couldn't believe this to be true. There must be an injustice and as I hated all authority figures it must be the headmaster who was in the wrong. As far as I knew, nobody had disclosed being the object of Mr Graveney's attentions, there were only rumours. I was also friendly with one or two other boarding masters, and short of asking a direct question, which I was scared to do, nothing was forthcoming from them.

The first disappearance was Ben Timbers, who one Saturday was seen packing his bags into his father's car. I can't say there was anything about him for me to miss. His combination of looks and personality was lethal.

At the end of the term the expected news came that Mr Graveney's contract had not been renewed. He had moved out a few days ago as he would not be accorded a fond farewell in the final assembly of the summer. He found a few minutes to stop and talk to me. I said how sorry I then genuinely was that he was leaving. He said he would be alright, and wished me the life I wanted for the future. He winked, and I winked back.

This story is part imagination, and I have put words in people's mouths. What do I think and feel looking back forty years?

My sixteen-year-old self had fallen helplessly and unrequitedly in love with my classmates, too reticent to make my feelings known. I knew I was not meant to be having them. Had an adult man approached me I would have been scared.

Mr Graveney. He was a young gay man. He may have been naive. Was he a paedophile? I cannot know whether the allegations which led to his dismissal were true. I think he was sexually attracted to adolescent boys, from the comments made by his Jack. Whether he acted on them is another matter. He never said "I fancy adolescent boys." I would query his choice of a boys' boarding school as a teacher. In my current profession I know that many paedophiles "find themselves" in jobs where they act *in loco parentis*: priests, teachers, choirmasters, care workers and, yes, scout masters. I say "find themselves" as they often deny even to themselves that their choices are underpinned by desires for sexual contact with the under-aged.

Ben Timbers. He was below the age of consent, but the author of most of the distress in what I've told you. If he was capable of casual violence and extortion at fourteen, I hate to think what he may have done since. I don't much like seeing sociopaths in my clinic, and I'd want no reunion with him. I remember that if he bothered to look at me I could see scorn in his eyes, as I had no sexual or other capital to desire or manipulate. Unfortunately, he was as gifted intellectually as he was criminally, and may now be some captain of industry, worshipped and feared.

Nineteen seventy-nine

Cartier Tank Americaine (model 1740) 18 Carat solid gold, 1991, Swiss, automatic movement. The name tank has been applied to watches with this shape of case (rectangular or square) apparently because of the similarity with the imprints made by the caterpillars of First World War tanks. Famously French, Cartier's watches such as this are now made in Switzerland.

The Smoke That Thunders

Mosi-oa-Tunya is Lozi for "The Smoke That Thunders". It richly describes the sight and sound of the Victoria Falls. The rainbowed spray can be seen from many miles away. It is also the name of Zambia's national brand of lager. Much spraying anywhere other than right in front of the bar goes on when a fresh supply comes to town. That said, when I lived there in a village in Luapula Province, trying to be an anthropologist, it wasn't the favourite commercial beer. That was smuggled over the Luapula River from what was then Zaire, now Democratic Republic of Congo. These beers had Swahili names. The pale golden one was *Simba* (lion) and the darker one was *Tembo* (elephant).

Countries are sometimes assessed by their alcohol-related habits. Thus all Celts are hopeless alcoholics while the English just shouldn't touch the stuff, ever. Southern Europe has beer for hot afternoons in bars, and wine to accompany food. To be drunk in public is shameful, rather than, as in England, an achievement. I'll get on to Zambia in a moment, but note for now I found parallels between Nordic and Zambian drinking habits. Back then in the 1980s I'd never been to Scandinavia so it wasn't until later I discovered it wasn't Zambia's fault that Scandinavians had a problem. I knew one Norwegian, three Swedes, and about ten Finns in Zambia. I think there's something about state control of alcohol supply which encourages paradoxical paralysis.

The Norwegian, like me, was an anthropologist. We were housed, with other postgraduate students, in student rooms at a place called

Marshlands, part of the University of Zambia. I spent my first month there before heading up country, and then came back about once every three months for a bit of city life.

The residents of Marshlands were a mixture of returning postgraduate Zambian students, mostly sane, and odd foreigners, some quite eccentric. One cowboy from Texas, complete with hat and boots, who was Jewish, spent time each evening parading the perimeter fence to block any holes a snake might get through. Given all the vegetation growing around the fence he was considerably raising his chances of being bitten. This behaviour didn't bode well as he was a herpetologist.

The bar at Marshlands hardly ever had anything to sell, and it was a long walk to the main campus. Instead we would ride via taxi or minibus to the throbbing heart of Lusaka, Cairo Road, and find a club or bar. At that time, not far away, was the far prettier, flowering tree-lined Saddam Hussein Boulevard. Iraq had given something to Zambia. It took until 2011 to change the name, imaginatively, to Los Angeles Boulevard.

We usually found ourselves in Moon City. About two-thirds of the women in there were with their pimps. I don't remember that much about one particular night apart from my wallet being lifted, but as expatriate men each of us got a land mine in the form of bulbous Zambian woman attaching to us. My Norwegian friend Bjorn had gone into cultural drinking mode by then. As anthropologist to anthropologist he tried later to say that the behaviour is a way of Norwegians getting over being naturally shy. It consists in becoming ruddily drunk and then starting to sing. Not like singing in Britain, but very serious back-slapping "folk" songs about the virtues of life. It was seriously friendly, not confrontational. Like the last night of the Proms with compulsory cocktails (many).

The prostitute who had attached herself to me was called Joy. I thought, if she didn't know, then no one else would about anything gay going on in Zambia. She asked me if Boy George was gay. Because I was not about to come out, I said I thought he might be. Then I asked her, ever hopeful, was there anyone gay here tonight. She said yes, there is one, but he's not here (I was used to Zambian English syntax) and he's a bit mad. He drinks too much. At this point in my residence in Zambia I knew this phrase was hard to interpret. Too much for what? An elephant? Intelligent life? Too much for other customers who couldn't get enough?

The night ended with us stumbling into another taxi. Bjorn with Ruth and Joy with me. I had not managed to shake her off. When we got back to Marshlands the two-metre metal gate had been locked. Shit, the taxi had gone and there were still four of us. The only way in was to climb. I can only say being twenty-five and in dread of a voracious female prostitute must have got me over. Despite being told how rude it was of me, I refused to pull Joy over after me. Bjorn went off with Ruth, and I got to my room joyless. I came out to Bjorn the next day after the hangover had gone. He found my dilemma hilarious.

My second month in Zambia found me waiting in the provincial capital, Mansa, while I sorted out my field placement. I could afford one night in the Mansa Hotel, followed by three weeks in an unspeakably unpleasant "Government Rest House" where I got bacterial diarrhoea, mosquitoes and cockroaches. I had one of those "What the fuck am I doing with my life" moments, an existential question we all face from time to time, but perhaps more frequent for anthropologists. Luck was on my side this time. While emptying

The Smoke That Thunders   181

my intestines in the hospital I met a Belgian volunteer doctor and I was soon connected to others volunteering in Luapula, and my good friends the Allens, who got me to my village and the start proper of my study.

Mansa showed me the next thing about national drinking habits in Zambia. There's a kind of bell curve of distribution of commercial beer, the further you get from the breweries (Lusaka and the Copperbelt towns in Zambia). Five years earlier I had lived in neighbouring Malawi. What they told me about Zambia was that it was very dangerous; they were all pissheads, and don't go near soldiers who've been drinking. Any interest in men in uniform was outweighed by the idea of pissed men with guns. I wasn't that stupid. If anything, more wariness was needed in Malawi. The comparison was an expatriate myth. The President for Life, His Excellency Dr H. Kamuzu Banda, was a strong leader who kept the nation safe, e.g. by having political opponents imprisoned or murdered. He had created a thuggish movement in the Malawi Congress Party called the Young Pioneers. Remind you of anything?

On a slow day I once read the Constitution of Malawi. It all seemed fair enough, until I noticed that after each clause was the rider, "Except in the case of the First President." This applied, for example, to general elections, which were free and fair and every five years but not allowed to happen. To give him his due, Banda did manage to stand down three years before dying in 1997. So technically he wasn't President for Life.

Being pissheads, as anywhere, is true of some Zambians. As in England, this often presents as bingeing en masse. The difference is supply and demand. That graph of two lines everyone gets taught in basic economics. In Britain the graph more or less persists. In Zambia the pattern is different. For what may be months the graph shows plenty of demand, but no supply. Then one day, the supply arrives. The graph looks normal. The day after – a blank page. No supply again, and briefly no demand. Thereafter back to lots of demand and no supply.

The drinking pattern is of course supply-driven. It's just that it's so stark. It's almost as if there is a fear that if bottled beer is not drunk immediately it will evaporate, be stolen, or spirited away by supernatural means. My experience was that Zambians and their friends would drink a bar dry every time beer came into town. On several occasions I had terrifying lifts home driven by one of the Finns or Zambian friends. Finnish drinking habits seemed close to Zambian, which didn't help, and I was terrified though drunk myself. By the end of an evening at the Mansa hotel you literally had to step over the bodies. Most of these were male. A few were female, who got labelled prostitutes because drunk women were shameful to men.

In the mists of time I can no longer remember if bottled beer ever came to the village bar. Something else did. A Southern African regional product which was drunk dry every time but for which replacement was much faster. In Zambia it is called Chibuku. It counts as beer, and is made from maize mash. I think there's a tight bell curve on its potability, which goes from innocuous to vinegar in a few days. As a visitor to a rural area this is what you are likely to be offered. As a village resident it would have been very rude for me to refuse. The problem was that I didn't like it. I really didn't like it. At its best, i.e. alcoholic but not yet completely rancid, my best description would be vomit, diluted with vinegar, and some bits of sweetcorn mixed in. This is not Chibuku's only challenge. If you Google it now it's presented in attractive packaging a bit like a milk tetrapak. In a village in Zambia in 1988 it arrived in what looked like a fuel tanker. That's probably what it

The Smoke That Thunders   183

was. It was pumped into some sort of vat in the bar, where it was open to the elements. It was served in five-litre plastic containers with the lids cut off, most of which had cooking oil in them previously (I hope). I think at most I managed half a container on any one evening and managed to chuck the rest somewhere else, usually in the squatteroo (my father's word for hole in the ground latrines, whether in the bush, France, or Islamic countries). It would end up down there anyway, why trouble my gastric tract with it, I thought. My attempts to lose Chibuku went largely unnoticed as very drunk people have limited observational skills. I would escape eventually by faking inebriation, and would be teased about not being able to take my drink. Of course I'd consumed some, but my Smoke That Thunders couldn't be described as a waterfall, nor that "scenes so lovely must have been gazed upon by angels in their flight" in David Livingstone's famous words. David Livingstone who, I reflected between farts, had died less than a hundred miles from where I squatted.

Right, I thought, I'm going to get my revenge on Chibuku. I was going on one of my quarterly R&R trips to Lusaka, to catch up with friends at the university and shop for things I couldn't get in Luapula. This time I went to the duty free shop, which only took foreign exchange. Some of my favourite things. Marmite – unaccompanied. Roquefort – have to eat it all at once and be sick. White Toblerone. Yes. I hadn't even known it existed until my friends Antonia and Michael pulled a bar from their freezer. Don't get drunk and put the marmite on it.

Alcohol. What to choose? I had been exposed to one other village product which was slightly less vile than Chibuku, but only a bit. This was made by women, and called wine, or waini in CiBemba. Wine technically described their product. It contained water, sugar and yeast. It was fermented. It's just that there were no grapes, or anything else, to give it flavour. The worst thing of all was that it reminded me

184 Watchwords

of my mother's attempts at homemade wine in the 1970s, which were universally awful. In chemistry lessons at school we had been shown how to make a still. Well, there was an illustration in the chemistry textbook. Dad, engineer, had the necessary parts, so with some aluminium tubing, a glass coffee percolator, a washing-up bowl of cold water and some corks I used Mum's wine to distil my first "vodka" at the age of fourteen. It was awful, but not as bad as Mum's wine. It may also have been nearer to methylated spirits than vodka. I'm still not sure why neither parent stopped me. Nor do I know if my own brew was as dangerous as what I would sample twelve years later in Zambia. I don't think Social Services had been invented in the leafy suburbs of Bristol in the 1970s.

In the duty free shop I settled on a couple of bottles of claret. I could give one out to share, and keep one for myself as there was zero chance of any coming back – unless it had already been drunk once. I was determined to use the example of France's gift to the world to show what shite the village women were making. This is *not* the way anthropologists are supposed to think. It's what they leave out of their writings. I also bought a bottle of Scotch for Mr Mongu, the agricultural project officer I worked with, who complained there wasn't enough strong liquor available. I should have remembered "enough" was not quantifiable where alcohol was concerned.

Back home in Chief Mabumba's village, and properly rested, I brought out my treasures. I'm not quite sure how it happened, but Mr Mongu managed to get hold of the wine as well as the whisky. He looked a little puzzled by the first sips of wine, so I left and said I'd return later. Just as the Zambian sun beautifully and quickly expired I found him again, two hours later. He was still ambulatory, just, but was cross-eyed and clearly more drunk than he thought he was. He didn't like the red wine. What the women made in the village was much better.

The Smoke That Thunders 185

The Scotch wasn't bad for a muzungu (white man's) drink. That's when I noticed he'd drained both bottles, and by the disappointed faces of those around, no one else had got a look in. He'd told them they were too uneducated for European drinks. Once you've got a job and a uniform in Zambia you can start calling your friends retarded, or retarded prostitutes if they're lucky enough to be women. Before passing out Mongu promised to take me for the local version of Scotch, but it was illegal so I mustn't tell anyone. The fifteen or so people in earshot all screamed with laughter, aieeeee.

"Don't worry, the next time I go to Lusaka I'll get you some tequila. You'll like it. Better than the Scotch. I'd get you some Thunderbird to wash it down, but I don't think the USA sends it here in their aid supplies. We'll need a plan to hide it from Mongu."

"We'll hide it in my pit latrine" said Tobias, a bit too quickly. I would rule that out as he was reputed to have died once already from alcohol.

"We need to put the alcohol into something even Mongu wouldn't think of."

Five minutes of concentrated thought.

"In my latrine." Tobias again. "I mean without the bottles."

There were two mind-altering substances I was aware of locally in the villages. Cannabis was scattered among the maize and cassava, some

186   Watchwords

distance from the roads. I smoked some a few times. Again the local experience was distinctive. First, the local tobacco was so lethally strong that even a heavy smoker might think twice. The second thing was that I never once saw papers for rolling cigarettes, except those imported by foreigners. So my occasional consumption of weed meant smoking a sort of cornet of newspaper. The being stoned only just about made up for the process of getting there, which was like simulating being in a house fire.

The other substance was kachasu, a very distant relation of cane spirit. This is a corruption, in both sense, of cachaça, the Brazilian cane spirit used in Caipirinhas. It must have come via the neighbouring Portuguese colonies of Angola and Mozambique. It's made by taking waini, or indeed any other source of alcohol, and distilling it. This is done by women who were known as shebeen queens. It is strictly illegal and there are recorded deaths from drinking it.

Mr Mongu took me and some other men friends on what I think was about a ten-mile walk into the bush. We arrived at a house on the edge of a village. There was talking from inside. A woman came out and gestured us in. I was in for a surprise. The loveliest experience I had of drinking in Zambia. This was a social, traditional drink, increasingly rare. We were to have a beer called Katubi, which is made from millet, a traditional crop now rare as it yields small amounts and can't command a market. The millet is ground and then fermented like a wine. When it is just right it is heated and poured into a large gourd calabash. The guests sit in a circle on the ground or stools around the calabash. The drink is supped through a reed, the reed being passed around the circle. We talked, we exchanged stories, we laughed. The flavour of the katubi was lovely, and I would say it was about the strength of wine. Even in a hot climate its warmth warmed the friendships. The nearest thing I can compare it to for anyone who

The Smoke That Thunders   187

hasn't had it is warm rice wine, sake. I can remember feeling very happy that day.

I would like to say that my model of Zambian drinking was put to rest by the day of katubi. I can't, but what I think is that the communal drinking of Katubi is the way things were, and what's there now is because of lifestyles, money, kinds of alcohol, ambitions. And unlike in England, when people get completely out of it on alcohol they don't seem to have fights as part of it. At least I didn't see any. Perhaps that's what the soldiers do. You won't be surprised to hear that the women only served.

Mr Mongu had one more treat for me. He'd deliberately let me think we were going to have kachasu on what turned out to be the katubi drinking trip. I liked the trick he'd played on me. Until. If the katubi trip had been Hogarth's Beer Street, then the final one was Gin Lane.

The scene that met us at the shebeen queen's was chaotic. One man was lying unconscious. Others were sloshing liquid out of their various tin mugs, gourds, plastic containers, and orifices. It was rowdy.

"There's lots of people here and they are quite noisy. Isn't there a problem with the police?" I didn't want to get PI'd (declared a prohibited immigrant) and sent home before I could finish gathering material for my PhD.

Someone pointed at the body on the ground and said "kabokala". I knew this meant police, but hardly needed telling as the man hadn't even bothered to get out of uniform before drinking.

I remember the kachasu was lethal. Rather like raki with the aniseed removed, in other words pure alcohol. It gave me my worst hangover ever the next day.

When you leave in Zambia you say something reciprocal on the lines of "stay well" – "go well". I knew enough Bemba now to recognise that someone had just said that the comatose policeman was the shebeen queen's husband. At this point I made my anthropologist's mistake.

It's no surprise that in learning languages very different from their own, anthropologists make mistakes, especially early in field work. Most of these mistakes are trivial and of no interest to anyone else. Occasionally they are hilarious. I've noticed the published hilarious ones often have something in common. This is that it's one particular English word which gets misplaced – cunt. I can't remember where it's from, but there's an example of some anthropologist somewhere on leaving his hosts saying "Your wife's cunt smells like fish" instead of "Your wife's cooking smells wonderful." I'm not sure I believe all of these stories.

My own mistake was that when I heard the policeman was married to the shebeen queen I said to her "Temûlume wandi" instead of "Mûlume obe". "He isn't my husband" instead of "He's your husband." An irony only known to me.

Now, having abolished alcohol from my life, returning to Zambia

The Smoke That Thunders   189

could be quite painful. A group I avidly avoided there before were the evangelical fundamentalist Christians, who might now might make the mistake of trying to embrace me as a teetotaller. In the 1980s one man in particular gave me conniptions, to the extent that when I attended his wedding I wrote a very rude poem about him and gave it to a friend. When Antonia reminded me of it many years later I couldn't remember it. I was probably pissed.

Omega men's dress watch with bullseye dial, stainless steel, 1954, Swiss, mechanical movement. This watch bears an inscription with delicately inscribed letters which can refer to an activity and also to persons currently in the public eye.

Dedication

We met outside Lamberwich Town Hall with bikes, as instructed by Thomas. He had been very vague on the phone about what he wanted help with. I knew it had something to do with a vintage watch. I asked if he was a collector and he said no. He did, though, need to find something very special for someone else, which was to be presented on a public occasion. I was puzzled. Thomas often seemed to have no filter between brain and mouth, so the secrecy and taciturnity were odd. A change, but I couldn't tell if good.

I was a watch collector myself and regularly visited one of the few vintage watch makers left in Central London. For reasons unclear to me we had to cycle, so the two of us wobbled off on our Metro Bikes. It certainly wasn't that Thomas was an experienced cyclist; a bystander might have thought we had a suicide pact. We managed to cross the river, then head west towards Clerkenwell. The shop was just off Saffron Hill.

"I'm not coming in," said Thomas. "I mustn't be recognised."

"This is getting more bizarre, Thomas. So what do you want me to do?"

"I want you to go into the shop and find something vintage which would make a special present. And I would like to have the following engraved on the case." He scribbled down two initials. "I'll wait for you outside."

192   Watchwords

"Just that?"

"Yes, and you can spend up to a thousand pounds."

"It must be for a very special occasion and person."

"At least one of those," replied Thomas.

I left both bikes with Thomas and buzzed myself in.

"Hello, Paul," said Joel. I liked Joel. I had expected all watchmakers to be blind curmudgeons who forgot where they put things, hinting at dementia. Joel was in his thirties and only rude for fun (I think).

"Haven't seen you in a while."

Joel was wearing his watchmaker's magnifiers so he looked like a character in a Tim Burton movie about to do something nasty, perhaps to an animal.

"Oh, hello there." There was Cat, his gamine assistant, getting up from replacing the watch trays. "Nice to see you. We haven't had a natter in a while."

Dedication   193

"I'm going to amaze you, Cat. I've come in to buy something. Something special."

"Blimey, I'm gobsmacked," said Joel. "I think you owe me, say, three thousand quid for saving you from expensive mistakes on eBay."

"Who's it for?" asked Cat.

"I don't know."

"That's helpful."

"It's a presentation watch."

"That's even more helpful. How can you have it engraved if you don't know who it's for?"

"The person who's buying the watch has asked me to have two initials put on it."

"Wouldn't it be easier for the buyer to come in himself, like a normal person?"

"He says he mustn't be recognised by anyone. But he's nearby if we need to do any dealing."

Cat just raised her eyebrows; Joel spoke. "Okay, so you're the counsellor for these people. Rather you than me. Have you *any* idea what he's looking for?"

"I'm going to go by what I'd choose for myself. I would say something from the 1950s. Preferably gold, but stainless steel would be fine. As for make, I'd go for Longines, Omega, possibly Jaeger Le-Coultre. Not Rolex, that would be too expensive."

"And what about the dedication?" I showed Joel and Cat the piece of paper. They both laughed out loud.

"Are you absolutely sure that's what you want?"

"Not me, my colleague."

"Well," said Joel, "have a look through what we have in stock. If you pass stage one of task weird I'll show you the choice of lettering you can have for your special message."

Just as Cat began to get out the trays of watches, Max, the assistant watchmaker, came back from lunch. They regaled him with my fool's errand, and he laughed too.

Dedication   195

"It's as well it's not an eighteenth birthday present," he said. "The recipient would die of embarrassment and never forgive his parents." Then he stopped in his tracks. "Do you remember that man who came in the other day with the 1950s Omega? He wanted to sell it because the dedication was a secret message from his lover who had recently died. Nutty as a nut of course. I think the initials are the ones you're looking for."

"Yes, I think it's over there in that drawer," said Joel. "I think we were going to polish out the dedication. Paul, you might be doing us a favour this time. Less work for us."

I went and gestured to Thomas through the window. He wouldn't come in.

"Can I just go and show it to him through the door?"

"Yes. Do you want to take some of our other watches at the same time?" said Joel. "Hand them out?"

I showed the Omega to Thomas. "Perfect, Paul, how much?" He seemed genuinely excited.

"Ah, I hadn't asked. Oh, and we'll get a discount as I'm a regular customer."

"Doesn't matter, here's some cash."

Thomas handed me a thousand pounds in notes.

"Don't you feel unsafe carrying all that cash around?"

"Strictly cash, it mustn't be traceable." Now I was feeling worried.

Joel let me have the watch for £875 in a nice presentation box.

Thomas let me keep the change, shredded and threw away the receipt and we pedalled our way back to Lamberwich Town Hall.

We sat and had coffee in the restaurant. Thomas had first consulted me as a counsellor when he believed he might be autistic. At the time I was prepared to entertain this as a possibility, though the personality traits always seemed to disappear when you looked for them. Now I was plain flummoxed.

"I think we have exactly what I need," said Thomas, "and thanks for all the help, Paul. I wouldn't have known where to begin."

"Thomas, I'll be straight with you, I'm beginning to feel we shouldn't have started this, whatever 'this' is. Can you tell me anything more about what it's all about?

Dedication 197

You've been behaving strangely, like you were moonlighting for the intelligence services or something."

"Well, okay, the watch is for presentation to a very senior member of staff for remarkable service to London, on his retirement. It's to be awarded on St George's Day."

"It's what?"

"That's what the others said. Bruno just replied, 'London's in England.'"

"Oh, it's for Bruno's retirement. So how can it be a surprise to him? I understand he drafted the plans himself for his big day."

"The occasion isn't the surprise. It's the present, and he absolutely mustn't know about it until the last moment."

England's patron saint's day came around. A group of journalists and detractors waited in the foyer for Bruno's arrival. I was in the inner sanctum, and I noticed there was no sign of Thomas. There were various speeches about the unique service the Mayor of Lamberwich had provided over the years. Then came the presentation. Grandiloquent, as I expected. After polite regrets from more senior and sensible invitees, the role of bestowing the parting gift had fallen to the Bishop of Upney. Something looking like a travesty of an Anglo-Catholic mass followed, the Mayor of Lamberwich on his knees ready not to receive a wafer but something rather larger. He rose, bowed to the Bishop, then moved to the lectern to make his speech. Some carelessly worded hyperbole from Bruno left everyone unclear as to whether they were being praised or insulted. He said he'd made a unique contribution. That was certainly true.

"I hope my successor carries on my good work. I have laid the foundations for a royal road to a truly remarkable borough, a peacock among crows in London. I see my greatest achievement in the encouragement of private enterprise for residential rejuvenation along the Thames. I leave you today, but my influence will continue. And I'm available for consultation at unreasonable rates." The laughter was almost drowned out by the booing outside. Bruno had arranged for loudspeakers to broadcast his message to the poor.

He looked at the object in his hand. He carefully opened the box and removed the Omega. It was beautiful; even Bruno could see this. There seemed to be some kind of label tied around it. The Mayor turned the watch over. On the label was written, "Over the years you clearly have not remembered who I am, Bruno. This is for all the times you made me do this for you at school. Thomas." Bruno lifted the label from the back of the watch. On the watch case were two exquisitely engraved initials – BJ. Stunned silence. A face at the back of the hall, just arrived, smiled in triumph.

Dedication   199

Acknowledgements

Watchwords would not have been possible without the
help of Jonathan Griffiths of Antique Watch Company,
Lizzy Burt who designed the book, and Jane Rogers
who was throughout my friend and editor.

In addition Katie Deverell, Alan Nadin, Ford Hickson,
Will Anderson, Mary Verdon and Philip Reilly acted
as critical readers.

Printed in Poland
by Amazon Fulfillment
Poland Sp. z o.o., Wrocław